Accomplice

Accomplice

Valerie Sherrard

DUNDURN PRESS

TORONTO

Editor: Shannon Whibbs
Design: Jesse Hooper
Printer: Webcom

Library and Archives Canada Cataloguing in Publication

Sherrard, Valerie
 Accomplice / by Valerie Sherrard.

Issued also in an electronic format.
ISBN 978-1-55488-764-4

 I. Title.

PS8587.H3867A74 2011   jC813'.6   C2010-902453-2

1   2   3   4   5   15   14   13   12   11

 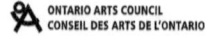

We acknowledge the support of the **Canada Council for the Arts** and the **Ontario Arts Council** for our publishing program. We also acknowledge the financial support of the **Government of Canada** through the **Canada Book Fund** and **Livres Canada Books**, and the **Government of Ontario** through the **Ontario Book Publishers Tax Credit** program, and the **Ontario Media Development Corporation**.

Care has been taken to trace the ownership of copyright material used in this book. The author and the publisher welcome any information enabling them to rectify any references or credits in subsequent editions.

J. Kirk Howard, President

www.dundurn.com

Dundurn Press	Gazelle Book Services Limited	Dundurn Press
3 Church Street, Suite 500	White Cross Mills	2250 Military Road
Toronto, Ontario, Canada	High Town, Lancaster, England	Tonawanda, NY
M5E 1M2	LA1 4XS	U.S.A. 14150

Prologue

Handcuffs are cold.

My name is Lexie Malton. I'm fifteen years old and I'm in the back of the sheriff's van, on my way to being locked up. You might think there would be some serious things to think about at a moment like this. But my brain has switched to some kind of freeze-frame mode. Only short flashes of information are getting through — like the coldness of the metal circling my wrists. At least they're cuffed in front of me. Any time I've seen the cops slap the cuffs on someone in a movie, it's always behind them. I bet that would be a lot more uncomfortable.

Not that comfort is my main concern right now.

My eyes slide closed as I try to block out the reality of where I am. It doesn't help. Sometimes what's in your head is worse than what's around you. Screams and gunshots, blood and sirens flood my thoughts.

I open my eyes again and look around for something to distract me. I lean to the side until I can see out the front window of the van. As I get my bearings, I realize that we're leaving the city behind. The city, my life, and my family. I can't stand to think about my father, or how his face crumpled when they put the handcuffs and shackles on me.

Yes, shackles, too. They feel surprisingly heavy around my ankles. I can't help but think that they weren't really necessary. I mean, even if I made a break for it, it's not like I'd get far. Having your hands cuffed doesn't exactly help your balance. I picture myself trying to run like that. There's no doubt I'd end up sprawled out on the ground. My captors probably wouldn't even have to break a sweat to catch me.

The image that comes to mind might even be funny if it wasn't for the trouble I'm in. So much trouble.

It's hard to believe that this morning started out just like any other day.

Chapter One

Three months earlier ...

The rain was too good to be true — plump drops splashing down like tiny water-bombs bursting. It lasted six minutes. I know this because the clock on the wall of a used bike shop across the street said 2:17 when it started. He was seventeen minutes late then, and twenty-three minutes late when it stopped.

I watch the after-rain steam coming off the street, hazy wisps rising up in the afternoon heat. It's been unbearably hot and humid, but the brief downpour hasn't done a thing to clear the air. If anything, it's worse. I feel like I'm breathing through a wet sheet.

I scrounge around in the printed canvas bag I have slung over my shoulder, find a nearly empty pack of gum and shove a piece through the green foil. As I chew it, I wish I'd thought to bring a few fresh packs and a couple of Mars bars with me. Things like that can buy five, even ten minutes with Devlin, before he evaporates like the afternoon's rain.

Another glance at the clock tells me that more than half an hour has now passed since I got here — and there's still no sign of him. It's okay that he's late. I just want him to show up. It's the only way I can be sure he's still alive.

People pass in and out of view. Every time I'm in this part of town I'm struck by how sluggish their movements are. Their slow, dragging feet seem to lack purpose — as if they're plodding forward with nowhere to go.

An older woman stares at me as she goes by. She looks puzzled. Maybe she thinks she knows me from somewhere, but there's something angry in her expression, too. When she moves past me I realize I've been holding my breath. It escapes in a rush and I gulp in air.

"Would you like to tell me why you aren't in school, young lady?"

I jump, startled, but the deep voice doesn't fool me for more than a split second. I turn to face Devlin, who has somehow managed to sneak up behind me.

A sloppy smile is splashed on his face. There was a time that my heart did a happy skip at that sight, but it's been a while since that happened. Now, my stomach clenches in a mixture of anger and guilt.

"Hey, Dev," I say, brushing away unpleasant thoughts.

"You have something for me?" The smile is still there, but it's already becoming thin and stretched. It reminds me of a super-villain, though I can't remember which one.

I know I'm doing the wrong thing. Enabling. Helping him destroy himself. I always start out saying "no," but it's not that easy to stick to it. He sounds so desperate when he calls. He begs and tells me I'm the only one who ever cared for him. He swears it will be the last time. He screams and says horrible things. He cries and talks about having nothing to live for. It just goes on and on and in the end I give in. Every time.

"Hey, c'mon," he says. "You have it or not?" His eyes dart around, but they keep coming back to my bag.

"I could only get ten," I tell him.

"Okay, so, give it to me." He's more jittery than I've ever seen him before. It's like his feet are rubber, the way he's bouncing up and down from foot to foot.

I reach into the bag and slide my fingers into the side pocket where the bill is tucked. The second my hand comes back into sight holding the money, Devlin reaches out, snatching it. A tremor passes through him. Anticipation.

"Thanks, Lexie. You're the best."

I feel like a fool. "It's okay," I tell him. "But remember — this is the last time. I mean it. Don't ask me again."

"Yeah, no problem." He's antsy now — itching to get out of there. I know the next thing he's going to say before it comes out of his mouth. "So, anyway, I gotta go."

He leans forward and kisses my forehead. It takes all of my resolve not to draw back from the smell of his unwashed clothes and body and hair.

He turns and walks away, his steps quick and eager in spite of the heat that's making everyone sluggish. From what I've seen, that's the only time you see someone move fast in this part of Vancouver — when they're going to score.

Devlin turns the corner, disappearing from sight. Not until he's gone do I start to move, making my way toward the Skytrain station. It's the seventh time I've come to this part of town. Now, for the seventh time I promise myself it will be the last.

Even if it wasn't wrong to give Devlin money, I know I shouldn't be walking around in this part of the city. I don't feel safe here. The thought pops into my head that my step-mother, Andrea, won't even drive *through* this neighbourhood.

I picture what her pointy little face would look like if she knew I was in the East Hastings area, instead of at my desk at Killarney Secondary. It's almost enough to make me smile. But when I glance up, I'm jolted back to the here and now.

A group of half a dozen guys who are probably in their late teens or a bit older are converged at the intersection just ahead. I see at once that they're wearing colours. My stomach knots as they catch sight of me and turn in my direction.

Scanning the buildings ahead for somewhere to duck doesn't offer much hope. First up is a Laundromat that's so run down I'm not even sure it's open. There's no way it's staffed. The storefront past that is boarded up and sporting a sign advertising it for sale or lease.

On the other side of the street is a small pawn shop with bars in its windows. The sign in front says it's open. After fighting the urge to turn and run in the opposite direction, I figure that it's my best option.

I'm halfway across the street when the gang members make their move.

Chapter Two

The slow, deliberate way they start toward me is somehow scarier than if they were running. It says they're confident — that there's no need to hurry because they *know* they'll catch me.

My heart is pounding so hard that I can hear the blood roar in my ears. I'm almost to the pawnshop by then but it now seems like the stupidest place I could have picked to go. I hear a muffled shout to my left, followed by laughter.

I stumble slightly at the edge of the sidewalk, but regain my balance before it's too late. Sweat runs into my eyes and my shirt clings damply to my back. Then I'm at the door, taking hold of the handle and yanking it open. Even in this state of panic, the cool air that blasts over me is a welcome relief. I blink as my eyes adjust from the bright glare outside to the indoor light.

An old woman is looking at me from behind a display case where she's seated. Great. She'll be a lot of help, I'm sure.

"Excuse me, ma'am, is there a back way out?" I ask, trying to stay calm so I won't frighten her.

She shakes her head slowly while I glance back and forth between her and the plate glass window. The gang has almost reached the store. One of the guys breaks into a huge grin as he catches sight of me standing there. He says something to the others and they all look in and laugh.

They're almost at the door … and I'm trapped! I try to think, but it's as if my brain is frozen. The squeaky sounds of the old lady's voice float across the room to me, but I can't make out the words. It doesn't matter, anyway. I can neither move nor speak.

They're here! But they don't turn toward the door. I watch in disbelief as they just keep walking. Convinced it's a trick, I step a little closer to the door and peek out. They're moving farther away, talking among themselves.

Relief rushes through me. My knees threaten to give out. I reach for the nearest display case and sag against it.

"You go! You go now!"

The poor old woman at the cash is looking at me anxiously. I try to explain, but I can see she thinks I'm stoned, or maybe crazy. She keeps waving her hands, shooing me out the door, I guess.

"Okay, okay. I'm going," I tell her. I figure, why upset the poor old thing? And anyway, it's easier than trying to persuade her that I'm no threat.

The blast of heat that hits me when I step back outside nearly knocks me over after the cooler air inside the pawnshop. I look to my left and see that the gang members are moving steadily away. As I watch them, one glances back over his shoulder and sees me there. He turns suddenly and makes a lunging move in my direction.

I jump and let out a little scream. By then, the others have turned and are watching. A great roar of laughter goes up from the group. One of them yells, "Boo!" which increases their amusement.

I smile sheepishly, wanting to show them that I'm a good sport. It's now clear to me that they were entertaining themselves at my expense, but I'm not kidding myself. It would be stupid to do anything that could make them angry.

The tallest of them lifts an arm in some kind of salute before they turn away again. I almost envy them for being able to move so fearlessly in this part of town.

It's just a couple more blocks to the Skytrain and I head there as quickly as I can through the stifling waves of heat.

It's a relief to reach the station at Main and make my way to the platform. A gentle rumble from the ground tells me a train is coming seconds before it bursts into view. It glides into the station and comes to a stop, its doors opening quickly for the exchange of passengers getting on and off.

I hurry on and sink into an available seat. My eyes close for a few moments as I try to shut out the day and its events. It doesn't work. Instead, I see Devlin's pale face — the loose smile and eyes that are focused so far away. I wonder if I might have imagined the times, not so very long ago, when it seemed those same eyes saw things in me that no one else ever had.

How did it all turn into such a complete mess?

And I wonder what Oscar would say if he knew where I was — and why. Most guys would totally flip out over something like that. And break up with me.

Oh, yeah, I have a boyfriend. I guess that makes it seem even stranger that I'm here, risking my neck to meet up with an ex. And giving him money.

First thing you'd think would be that I still care for Devlin. Well, I do, but not because there's a whole lot of lingering romance. I care about him as a friend and a human being. But mostly, I feel responsible for him. And guilty.

This kind of guilt is hard to shake. It eats away at me every day, like some kind of black worm gnawing through my insides. I can't shake it. I can't talk myself out of it.

A year ago Devlin was my boyfriend. He was also one of the school's star athletes, and a decent, if not great, student.

And then I did something that destroyed him.

Chapter Three

"Where were *you* this afternoon?"

I look up from my locker to find Oscar peering at me through the deep brown clump of hair that falls over his forehead. His expression is barely inquisitive and I wonder just how much he knows.

"What do you mean?" I ask. I keep my voice casual and go back to digging in my locker. I'd made it back to school about twenty minutes before the final bell and was hoping no one had noticed I'd been gone.

"I was looking for you at break and Vaughn said he saw you heading toward the side doors right after lunch. I thought maybe you went somewhere."

Vaughn is Oscar's twin brother. Fraternal, that is. They couldn't look any different if they tried. Oscar is tall and slim with dark hair and eyes. Vaughn is shorter and broader, with lighter hair and eyes that are washed-away blue-green.

"The side doors?" I say, like this is the first time I've heard of them. "Oh, over in history.

Yeah, I was down that way. Vaughn thought I was busting out, did he?"

The laugh I manage sounds a little off to me, but Oscar doesn't seem to notice. He shakes his head and shrugs.

"Whatever," he says. "No big deal."

I smile at him and sling my pack over my shoulder, but it bothers me — how good I'm getting at lying. Not just to Oscar, either. To my dad, and my sisters, too, and it doesn't even end there! Last week, I lied to my best-friend-since-grade-eight, Dori Tocher, when we were supposed to meet for Whoppers at BK and then go shopping for bathing suits. A frantic call from Devlin ended with me weeping and ditching Dori to take him fourteen dollars — which was the last bit of cash I had stashed away for emergencies.

It's getting out of control — I know it is. What I *don't* know is how to stop it.

Oscar walks at my side, oblivious to the thoughts churning in my head. I fight the temptation to confess, to tell him everything. For some reason, I can't seem to get that scene to play.

It makes me really start to wonder. What *would* Oscar say if I should suddenly admit that I've been sneaking off to meet up with Devlin, and taking him money?

I don't imagine he'd be thrilled, but I find I'm coming up blank trying to picture exactly how he'd react. That bothers me. Seems that I should be able to figure out how my boyfriend would take something like that.

The thought sneaks in that I'd have known with Devlin — I could predict what he'd do in most situations. I remind myself that Oscar isn't Devlin.

"Lexie?"

I realize Oscar has been talking and I haven't heard a word he's said. "Sorry," I tell him, "I guess I sort of drifted there."

"I'm getting used to that lately," he says.

"Sorry," I say again.

"I asked you if you want to come over. Mom's got a property showing or meeting or something, so she left some cash for us to order a pizza. There'd just be the three of us."

That's the only thing that's a bit strange about dating one of the Lee twins. Oscar includes Vaughn in our plans on a pretty regular basis. Sometimes I feel as though I'm dating both of them.

"I can't."

He shrugs, like it doesn't matter at all, but he doesn't look too happy.

"Sorry."

"Stop saying you're sorry about everything," he says, glancing down at me. "And don't ask me if I'm mad, either. I hate that."

"I wasn't going to ask you that," I lie. Inside, I'm pleased that he knew it.

"Right. Okay, so, I'll see you tomorrow then."

We've reached the stop and my bus is just pulling up. I board it and drop into a seat beside a woman who's clutching her purse on her lap. Oscar disappears out of sight as the bus lurches forward and rolls along Birch Street. I stop looking out the window and my eyes rest for a second on the woman next to me. She's staring ahead.

Strangers hardly ever talk to each other on the bus. They spend most of their time taking care not to make eye contact, pretending to be looking out the window or at their hands or the seat in front of them. Anything to avoid speaking.

Devlin, now, he'd talk to just about anyone. That's actually how we first started going out.

I'm admiring my nails, which Dori has just done for me with her French manicure kit. (This is back when Dori was going to be a nail artist and do celebs' nails in some sunny place.) It was a mature choice, going for the plain white tips instead of the glitzy nail art she always talked me into.

"*Know what they do when they declaw a cat?*"

I look up, surprised to see Devlin Mather facing me from the seat ahead.

"*People think they just take out the claws,*" he says without waiting for me to answer.

"*They don't?*"

"*Nope. It's brutal. They cut off the last bone — like if someone cut your fingers off at the last joint.*"

My fingertips curl into my palms and I shove my hands down to my sides. "*That's awful.*"

Devlin nods solemnly. "*You have any cats?*"

"*One,*" *I say.* "*Kramer. And he's not declawed, if that's what you're wondering.*"

"*Actually, I was wondering if I could meet him sometime.*"

"*You want to meet my cat?*"

"*I really do.*" He smiles and raises one eyebrow. "*So, when can I come over?*"

I laugh. "*You're weird,*" *I tell him.*

He just smiles and waits.

"*Saturday,*" *I say.* "*Saturday after lunch. You can come over then.*"

"*To meet Kramer,*" he says. His smile grows.

"*Yes, of course. To meet Kramer.*" *My insides are fluttering.*

"*I'll be there,*" he tells me, "*at 1:37.*"

Of course, that was the old Devlin, not the one who lives in his skin these days.

There are times when I think about him that it feels like someone is standing on my chest.

Chapter Four

The house is oddly silent when I get home. Dad and Andrea won't be off work for a couple of hours, but usually at least one of my sisters is home before me. Today, there's no sign of either of them.

Barb is seventeen and the oldest of the three of us, but she's low functioning. The best way I can explain what she's like is that she's sort of stuck at about ten years old. Most days Barb gets home from her special school first, but a few times a month they stay late for some kind of special event. Those are the only times she's late so this must be one of those days. Since the special-needs bus delivers her right to the door, she'd be here if her school was out.

Lynne is thirteen and we're fairly close, even though I'm three years older. We used to fight a lot, but things changed when Dad married Andrea a couple of years ago. After that, it got to be us against her. Andrea is about as two-faced as you can get. It didn't take us long to see through her act.

I probably sound like one of those kids who hang on to the hope that their parents will get back together, even though it's obvious that's never going to happen. That's not how it is. My mom died when I was seven. The doctors said it was an aneurysm. All I knew was that one day I had a mother and the next day she was gone. I haven't felt totally safe since.

I was actually kind of glad when Dad started to see other women. I knew he was sad a lot, plus I thought it would be awesome to get a new mom. I pictured someone teaching us to make cookies and doing cool mother-daughter stuff. Well, trust me, that's not Andrea. She's all about herself and her job.

She doesn't even *have* to work. My dad says so all the time when she complains about being tired and stressed. I'm glad she never listens to him, though. I'd hate to have to see her when I get home from school every day. The empty house I'm in at the moment is way better than that!

I'm not particularly surprised that Lynne isn't here. She's late getting home at least once a week. She's probably with a friend. Goodness knows she has a lot them — more than I do, that's for sure. Lynne has this happy way about her that makes people automatically like her.

I toss my backpack into the hall closet. It can stay there until Monday for all I care. Year-end exams are next week, but there's no point in trying to cram now. It's not like I'm going to flunk anything; who cares about great marks?

I make a stop in the kitchen where I spread peanut butter on half a dozen crackers then grab a bottle of Gatorade and head to the TV room. I sit there nibbling and staring at the screen without actually registering what's on.

Kramer appears from nowhere, lured, no doubt, by the sound of snacking. He purrs loudly and jabs his head into my leg to let me know he's there.

"Okay, okay." I reach down to scratch behind his neck and offer him the last cracker. He sniffs at it and gives me a haughty look. I pop it into my mouth whole and go to the hall closet where we keep a ridiculously large assortment of cat snacks.

I scatter some crunchy treats on the floor. He's munching on them as the front door opens and Lynne comes in.

"Thanks for nothing!" she yells at me.

"You're welcome," I say. The stony look she gives me tells me she's not amused. I vaguely wonder what I've done. Lynne's not the sort to keep things bottled up — so I figure she's about to tell me.

Except she doesn't. Instead, she bursts into tears and runs down the hall to her room. A trail of words I can't make out follows her, ending with the slam of a door. I feel a pang of guilt, but manage to turn it into anger within minutes.

"You'd think she was ten instead of thirteen," I mutter to myself. "What a baby. Besides, it's not like I don't have enough on my mind without having to deal with *her* outbursts."

It's not until Dad and Andrea get home and we're all sitting down to dinner — Kraft Dinner and wieners, one of the three things Barb has mastered for when it's her turn to cook — that I find out what was upsetting Lynne.

"So, Lynne," Dad asks, swiping a hunk of wiener through a blob of ketchup and holding it up in midair, "how was the great shoe hunt today? You and Lexie do much damage to my Visa?"

Oh, yeah. Dad had given me his credit card and I was supposed to meet Lynne at the mall. I wonder how I could have forgotten that. She'd been so excited about getting new shoes to go with her dress for the year-end formal. It's all she's talked about for weeks.

I turn to tell her I'm sorry, but her expression stops me cold.

"*Lexie* didn't show up." Lynne's words are clipped and hostile and perfectly matched to the look she's giving me. "And since *she* had the credit card, I couldn't go, even though An-mei said she'd go with me."

"What happened, Lex?" Dad's eyebrow is raised as he looks over at me.

"I forgot, okay?" I pull the Visa card out of my back pocket and hold it out to him, but he doesn't reach for it.

Instead, he rubs his forehead with his fingertips, pushing the skin into folds. I'm expecting a lecture any second, but it's Andrea who speaks up.

"Can you go with Lynne tomorrow?"

"I guess," I shrug.

"I'd take her myself, but I have to go in to work," Andrea says. I'm amazed that she doesn't mention something about her big assistant manager position and all the responsibility she has. It's just a stupid job in a women's clothing store, but you'd think she was running the space program the way she goes on about it.

"Maybe I'd like to make my *own* plans sometimes," I say, "instead of always getting stuck looking after Lynne."

"See how she treats me?" Lynne whines.

"There's no need for you to use that tone with Andrea. And I really don't think it's asking too much of you to help out now and then,"

Dad says. I can see he's on the verge of blowing his stack.

"What's the big deal? I *said* I'd do it." I push back from the table and walk away. Halfway to my room I change my mind and head for the front door. I grab my bag and ease the door open quietly.

"I'll be back in a while," I yell. I dash out the driveway and go left under cover of the Pitlanskys' fence. The corner is only a couple of houses away, and as long as I can make it there before anyone catches me, I'm pretty much home free.

I can hear Dad calling my name just seconds after I turn onto 41st. His tone tells me he's not coming after me, so I slow my pace and try to get my breath. I'd forgotten, in the cool inside the house, how sweltering it is, and my face and neck are already covered by a sheen of sweat.

I flip open my phone and press the button to dial Oscar. He answers on the second ring, his voice muffled. I can tell he's eating.

"I'm coming over, okay?"

"Sure." He sounds really glad.

I tell myself that I am, too.

Chapter Five

I feel better. A lot better. Oscar has his arm across my shoulder, his hand curled around my arm. He squeezes me closer to him every now and then, and smiles, and leans in to press his nose against my cheek or smell my hair. I can feel his happiness and it's spreading itself over me.

Vaughn's on-again-off-again girlfriend, Niki Chan, is there, too. Looks like they're on at the moment, which suits me fine. Not that I'm exactly friends with Niki. I know her from chemistry class in a casual, "hi-how-are-you" kind of way, but that's about it. Her family has money, which is actually the cause of most of the problems between her and Vaughn. He insists on paying his own way and she says there's no reason she should have to miss out on things she wants to do because of his pride — especially when she can easily afford to pay for both of them. It pretty much goes around in circles from there. But that's none of my business, and, in any case, I really don't care.

Vaughn and Niki are playing the latest *Metroid* game on Wii. She's bouncing and whooping while Vaughn makes do with assorted grunts and yelps. I've never been any good at these things — I panic and get jammed up.

Devlin loved the *Halo* games and used to coax me to play until I gave in a few times and he saw just how bad I really was.

It hits me suddenly that Devlin had been playing Xbox when Dad dropped me off at his place that night.

"I won't be too much longer," he'd told me. I'd dropped into the couch and picked up a magazine from the coffee table, flipping through it while he played, trying to hide my impatience.

It hadn't taken long for boredom to become annoyance. I made this known to Devlin in an escalating series of sighs and mutterings until he could no longer ignore me.

"You should try playing one more time."

"No. I hate those stupid games."

"C'mon Lex, just give it another shot. You'll love it once you get into it."

"No."

It echoed in my head now.

"No." Arms crossed. Anger stamped on my face. *"I want to go somewhere for a change. We never do anything."*

I wonder how I'd forgotten that detail. In all the times I've gone over it in my mind, not once had that hit me before now. What if I'd said "yes"? What if I'd picked up the controller he'd been holding out to me, and just played for a while?

Then we probably wouldn't have gone out that night, and run into Melissa Babineau and Cayla Forbes on their way to Jayden Dolan's place.

"You two should, like, totally come, too," Cayla had urged. "This is, like, *the* party of the year. Seriously."

I'd never been to Jayden's place before, but I'd heard about the parties. Who hadn't? His folks were always going on business trips or holiday weekends, leaving Jayden with an older brother who couldn't have cared less what Jayden did. From what I'd heard, he'd throw a big party and then call a service to clean up the next day.

Devlin wasn't exactly keen to go, but it hadn't taken much persuading. It was easy for me to talk Devlin into just about anything. He always wanted to please me.

"You never want to do anything fun!"

I feel sick, remembering the way I'd whined and pouted until he gave in — just like I knew he would.

Sounds and images tumble through my brain. They've been there before, the blurred colours and muted lights, crowded rooms and pulsing music.

It creeps forward, playing at its own speed.

Flushed faces and rowdy chanting. Jell-O shooters and clapping. Whoops and cheers and laughter. The cool, sweet taste of strawberry sliding down my throat.

Someone barfed bright red all over a cream-coloured carpet. It cleared the room, but no one seemed worried about it other than not stepping in it. I don't know why, but I felt oddly responsible, like I should do something about it. It was around this time that things started to spin and stretch. Still, I clung to the idea like it was a special mission.

It took a while to find Jayden — partly because the house is enormous and partly because things were getting pretty bleary. I kept asking kids I knew if they'd seen him, but most of them just stared at me. You'd have thought they had no idea who Jayden even was.

When I finally located him I found myself mumbling something confused about cleaning the spot on the carpet. It took a few minutes before he understood. Then he laughed.

"This is a party," Jayden said. "Who cares about a carpet? Just chill."

Then he was looking over my shoulder, at Devlin. "She always this uptight, man?"

"I'm not uptight!" I insisted, before Devlin could say anything. Not that it looked like he was about to. If anything, he was more wasted than I was.

"Oh, I think you are." Jayden smirked. "But you can prove me wrong if you want. If you're not too uptight, that is."

Chapter Six

You could never call Lynne a grudge-holder. By the next day she's dancing around the house with her arms around an imaginary partner, just as happy as can be.

"Do you think it's hard to dance in stilettos?" she asks, pausing in mid-twirl.

"Never tried it," I say, "but why take a chance? Besides, Dad would lose it if you came home with stilettos."

"'Cause I'm still his baby," she giggles. "So, what time do you want to go shopping?"

"Soon. I'm going to see if Dori can come, too," I tell her. I know there'll be no objection. Dori has more fashion sense than anyone I've ever known. I swear, she could put together a hot look with string and Kleenex if she had to.

Lynne continues dancing about while I dial Dori's place. Her mom tells me she's over at A.J. Ryan's house.

"Dori's at her boyfriend's place," I say, hanging up. Lynne looks so disappointed that I call his house.

"I'm looking for the famous fashion consultant, Dori Tocher," I tell A.J. once he comes to the phone. "Have you seen her, by any chance?"

"That depends," he says. "Are you trying to lure her away from me?"

"Absolutely."

"And is there a mall involved in this plan?"

"Maybe more than one."

"It's not looking so good for me then, is it?" he says with a groan, but he's kind of laughing, too. He's pretty awesome — I can see why Dori's so nuts about him.

"You can come along if you want," I offer.

"No, that's okay," he says quickly. "Uh, here's Dori."

"Shoes," I tell her. "For Lynne's dance."

"Where will I meet you?" she asks without missing a beat. Poor A.J.

Forty minutes later we're browsing at Shuzy Shoos, a new shoe store that carries "alternative styles," whatever that's supposed to mean. It's not like other shoe stores only have one style, but whatever. Lots of slogans are dumb when you think about them. I wasn't in love with the store name, either. Really, isn't it enough to spell "shoe" wrong once?

Lynne is looking at a pair of pointy-toed high heels while Dori watches over her shoulder, shaking her head.

"You want to have a good time or spend the evening limping around in pain?" Dori asks. "I'm telling you, you'll die in those things."

The salesgirl moves in. "How long is your dress?" she asks.

Lynne is answering her when my phone rings. The screen shows me an unfamiliar number. I answer.

"Lexie?" It's Devlin.

"What?" I move away from Dori and Lynne, even though neither one is paying the least attention to me.

"I need help, Lex." His voice is thin, a wire pulled tight.

"I helped you *yesterday*."

"I know, but it wasn't very much."

A surge of fury pulses through me. I step out of the store, where my voice won't carry to Lynne and Dori. "Yeah?" I say. "It wasn't very much? It was everything I could get, and I ditched school to bring it to you."

"You said you'd get twenty, but you only brought half. So, you kind of owe me the rest."

I shake my head, wondering how he managed to get things so twisted. Twenty was what *he'd* asked for the day before. It wasn't like I'd offered it. And now he was acting like I'd stiffed him.

"I got what I could get," I say. I can hardly keep myself from yelling. "And you have to stop calling me."

"Who else am I gonna call?"

"I don't' know. Nobody. You've got to get *help*."

"That's why I'm —"

"No! That's *not* why you called me." I notice I'm drawing stares from people walking by. I take a deep breath and lower my voice. "You called to ask me for money — *again*, but I don't have any money and anyway, I'm not helping you kill yourself anymore. I can't take this."

"Listen," his voice is frantic. Scared and frantic. "Just *listen* to me for one minute."

I know I should hang up. I tell myself it's what I need to do. But I can't, because what if he doesn't have another quarter and can't call back? What if he's somewhere, alone and suffering, and he doesn't even have anyone to talk to?

"I'm hurting bad, Lexie. I just need something to get me through this and then everything will be different."

"What? What will be different?" I can hardly believe I'm giving him a chance to tell me more lies.

"I'll go to rehab."

"You're lying. You say that every time we have this argument, and you never go."

"I mean it this time, I swear. I don't want to live like this anymore."

I say nothing. Dev takes my silence as a sign that I'm weakening. But the truth is, a terrible feeling of tiredness has settled on me. I can't find the energy to argue with him.

"So, try to get twenty this time — more if you can." His voice gets light and hopeful as he continues. "Hey — you know what? If I had fifty bucks I could get enough to wean myself down so I could handle rehab. That's why I haven't gone before — I was scared of how bad the withdrawal would be. But if I could ease off the stuff first —"

Lies, lies, and more lies. His and mine — they're all starting to run together.

He's still talking when I pull the phone away from my ear and press the power button.

Chapter Seven

That isn't the end of it, of course. There are more phone calls over the days and weeks that follow. More than once I am on the verge of giving in, of going to him. At those times, it's almost as if he can feel me weakening. He tells me I'm the only person in the world he really loves, the only one he can count on.

"No one else understands me," he sobs, his words blurred by the need and pain running through his body.

Other times I am stronger. He senses this and his attack on my will changes.

"Why do you hate me?" he sobs, when this seems the most likely way to pry open the door guarding my willpower. "You were the *one person* I thought still cared about me."

The self-pitying things he says rarely last long. He hasn't the patience to work it through, and instead, erupts in anger. He offers to smash in my face, to defile my mother's grave, to spread degrading stories about me. These threats are mindless words that force their way up from a howling ache for drugs.

Sometimes threats are followed by contrition, but more often his voice grows ever darker, uglier. Then, the words dissolve into babbled bits that I am glad I cannot decipher.

I learn that there is nothing he won't say, no emotion he won't use, no threat he won't make, to get what his body craves.

Often, his last-ditch effort is the one threat that truly scares me.

"I can't stand it," he whimpers. "Honest, Lexie, I can't take this. When I hang up, I'm going to kill myself."

But I hang on, somehow. I try to sound unmoved, even as my heart beats cold with fear.

"You're already killing yourself," I say, "and I'm not helping you do it."

Slowly, it gets a little easier to say no, and even to hang up. The guilty feelings are still there, but at least I'm not feeding them with more things to feel bad about.

The school year comes to an end and I start a summer job at Subway. I'm a "sandwich artist." Woo hoo! What a glam job. It's been an eye-opener, let me tell you! Businessmen in expensive suits try to charm us into little freebies: an extra meatball, more cheese, double bacon. Worse are the fussy women with pinched faces. They're never happy no matter how carefully you follow their neurotic instructions.

"Oh, dear — the olives aren't spread out very evenly, now, are they?"

"I'm *so* sorry, ma'am. I should have realized how traumatizing it would be if one bite had more olive in it than another. Here, let me arrange them in a symmetrical pattern. The people waiting in line behind you won't mind a bit."

Okay, those are the things you'd *like* to say, but never do. Not if you want to hang on to your fabulous career as a sandwich artist. And I did. After years of sharing one ancient computer with everyone in the house, my mind was made up. I was going to get a laptop of my own — something sleek and fast.

It takes no time to realize that saving money is harder than I expected. For one thing, working actually *costs* money! Shoes that are still comfortable after you've been on your feet for eight hours. Bus fare and lunches at work and clips so your hair won't look totally lame tied back. These things add up.

And what's the point of working if you don't have a little extra spending money? Oops. Did I say "extra"? That was a mistake. The first thing Dad and Andrea did when I got a job was sit me down and tell me they were proud of me. Oh, and that now that I was working I shouldn't expect any more handouts for movies and make-up and a whole long list of things I was now responsible for buying myself.

It's a wonder I don't go in the hole! If I'd still been giving in to Devlin, I would for sure. But he was getting the message, at last. Or so I thought.

The calls have almost stopped, but it's still not completely over. There's one horrible scene where he shows up at my house. The worst part is — Oscar is there.

It's Saturday evening and we've just been hanging out, listening to the new Roman Dane CD and talking idly about renting a movie. Dad and Andrea are gone to a party — something to do with her job, so you can just imagine how lame it is. Lynne is staying at a friend's place, but Barb is home, which means I can't go anywhere.

Then there's this knock at the door. It starts out loud and gets louder: Bang! *Bang*! BANG! Barb comes running down the hall from her room and throws herself onto the couch beside me. Her face is wide and scared.

"Lexie, someone's banging on the door," she says. "It's really loud."

"It's okay," I tell her. But I don't go to answer it. I'm glad Oscar is here, already on his way. "Look through the peephole to see who it is first," I tell him.

There's more banging. I hear Oscar mutter something, but I'm not quite sure what it is. Then he's back, standing there looking at me.

"It's Devlin Mather," he says. He shakes his head. "He looks bad. What do you want me to tell him?"

I'm instantly afraid, like something cold has just grabbed me. "I'll go talk to him," I say. "Can you stay here with Barb so she won't be nervous?"

"Yeah, but are you sure you'll be okay?"

I wave away his concern and head for the door. When I get there, I open it and step outside. I nearly push Devlin over because I'm in a panic to shut the door behind me. I don't know what he might say. If he brings up something about me taking him money — well, you can imagine what Oscar would think if he heard that.

As Devlin straightens back up I can hardly believe that it's him. He's looked worse every time I've seen him, but now the downhill slide has been fast and horrible. His face is blotched with sores and his eyes are like black holes in their sockets. Dirty clothes hang from his frame — once athletic, now thin and trembling.

I'm flooded with sympathy and disgust at the same time.

"Dev," I say, gently — kindly. My hand starts to stray toward his arm, but it doesn't get there. I can't bring myself to touch him.

"I need some money," he says. He leans in to speak and his breath is horrible. It's like he's rotting from the inside out.

I shake my head. "I can't," I say.

"You *can't*? You mean you *won't*!" He takes hold of my arm, squeezing it in anger. "You used to care about me."

"I still care about you," I say. I wonder if there's any truth left in the words.

"Yeah? That's why you stopped helping me?" His face is ugly with anger. "Do you know what I've had to do since you turned your back on me? The *things* I've had to do?"

He looks away for a few seconds but his eyes return to me. "Disgusting things, Lexie," he says. He covers his face with shaking hands. "But now, look at me. The cars don't even slow down."

A wave of nausea washes over me. I want to tell him I'll give him some money — just so he'll leave. But I know if I do, he'll be back, again and again.

"I'm sorry, Devlin," I say, forcing the words out. "I can't help you. You need to go to a rehab —"

His hand darts out and takes hold of my arm

a second time. The grip is tight and it hurts.

"I want that ring back," he says.

I stare at him.

"The ring I bought for your birthday. I want it back."

I can't quite believe what I'm hearing. He wants me to return a ring he gave me as a gift when we were dating. It's pretty — my birthstone set in a flower — and I really like it. For a second, I consider offering to give him whatever bit of money he'll get when he sells it. But somehow, I know that if I do that, he'll find a reason to come back for it again.

"Okay," I tell him. "You can have the ring." I look him straight in the eye, wanting him to see the contempt I feel. "Is there anything else you *gave* me that you want back?"

He gives it a second or two of thought. "No, that's it," he says, "just give me the ring." He wipes his mouth, leaving a trail of wet on the back of his hand.

I tell him to wait there. But I don't trust him to stay outside. I lock the door behind me when I go in. "I'll just be a sec," I call out to Oscar as I hurry down the hall to the bedroom I share with Lynne.

The ring is in my jewellery box. I grab it and go back to the door. This time I don't step outside.

"Here," I say, thrusting the ring toward Devlin. "But this is it. If you ever come back here, I'll call the police."

His teeth clench as he snatches the ring from my hand. He turns to go without a word, his movements jittery as he hits the sidewalk.

I try to convince myself that this is finally the end.

Chapter Eight

It's almost a month before I see Devlin again. Even so, the thought of him haunts me. I relive our last meeting over and over, wondering if I could have handled it differently.

To my relief, it didn't cause any problems with Oscar. Maybe that was because I was honest, for a change. When Oscar asked me what Devlin had wanted, I'd been on the verge of telling him yet another lie. It had been a surprise, then, when the truth came out of my mouth. Not the whole truth — just the truth about the ring.

"That's too bad," is all Oscar said. "I hope he gets straightened out."

Dori is a lot more inquisitive when I tell her about the whole thing the next day.

"No *way*," she says.

"It's true."

"Well, I know that. I mean, I know you're not making any of this up." She finishes applying polish to her nails and waves her hands about to speed up the drying. "It's just so hard to believe that Devlin would do something like that. I used to be a bit jealous of you, because he seemed so awesome."

"It's not *him* anymore," I say. "It's the addiction."

Dori gives me a long, steady look. One eyebrow goes up. "You guys broke up over this, right?"

"Yeah." I try not to think about the break-up. It still sits with me, the humiliation of seeing how easily I lost when I told him it was me or the drugs.

"So, what would happen if he got off it?" Dori asks.

"What do you mean 'what would happen?'"

"Would you go back out with him?"

"I'm going out with Oscar," I point out.

Dori rolls her eyes. "Like I don't know that," she says. She blows on her nails and then touches one with a fingertip ever so gently. "But what if Dev was clean again, and you had to pick. Would you stay with Oscar or go back to Devlin?"

"I don't know," I say. An image of Devlin, before drugs, flashes through my mind. It makes me want to cry, so I push it away. "I really loved Devlin, but a lot of bad things have happened. My feelings have changed — I don't think it could ever be the same again."

"How do you feel about Oscar?"

"I really don't know. He's a totally great guy and everything, but it's kind of strange. It's like I'm on the outside watching sometimes, like it's someone else going out with him, not me." I search for the words to make it clearer, but all I can come up with is, "I'd never want to hurt him."

"I bet it's hard for you to get close to Oscar because of what happened to Devlin," Dori says.

"Maybe."

She shrugs. "'Course, I'm no shrink," she adds.

"You know what — I already kind of suspected that," I laugh, "on account of the fact that you're still in grade eleven."

She swats at me for teasing her and then, thankfully, the conversation moves on. It stays in my head, though. I find myself wondering about it more and more.

What if Devlin *did* get clean? What if he went back to being the guy he used to be? Is that even possible?

I know he's been through a lot in the time he's been on the street. I fight them, but awful images push through sometimes. Devlin, putting himself at the mercy of men who use minors. I want to cry when I think of it. How does it feel to him, when he's clutching those few dollars for heroin? And, what other horrors has he been through? I try not to let myself think of what else he might have been willing to do for drug money.

How could he ever be the same, sweet Devlin I once knew? I know there's hope. There's always hope no matter how bleak things seem. I just don't know how much of him is left under that pale and sickly skin.

Guilt nags at me over the next while. I'm spending too much time thinking about Devlin. The disgust I felt at his last visit has faded. So many of the things I've been through and felt since the beginning have drifted off.

I can chart Devlin's whole journey to where he is today. It's a map of emotions, a road I never expected to walk. And I put us on it.

There was the beginning. The unease — just a hint of worry. I remember how he laughed that off. I remember his exact words.

"*Whaddya think — I'm going to turn into some kind of junkie?*"

I don't think I believed that could really happen — not then. The idea was impossible, at first. It didn't take very long, though. Was it months … or only weeks? I can't recall. I just know it happened so fast.

Worry became fear. Real fear. The kind that grips you and leaves you feeling cold and helpless. And anger. There was a lot of that, during those early days, before he was on the street. There were tears and pleading — the desperate kind where you cry and beg on your knees with your heart breaking.

None of it mattered.

None of it made the slightest difference.

In the beginning he lied. A lot. He hid things. He stopped being sweet and kind. Things disappeared when he was around. The one thing he never did was stop.

And now, when he's reached such a low place, I've forgiven him all of it. Somewhere inside, I know that he had to go down this far, if there was even a chance for him to come back up.

I'm tormented and exhausted. It's an effort to go through every day trying to act normal.

I realize, at last, that I'm waiting for something.

And then it happens.

Chapter Nine

It's Devlin's mother who calls to tell me. Seeing the familiar number on the phone and hearing her voice freezes me in place. I can barely breathe for the fear squeezing my chest.

"Lexie?"

"Yes," I manage. The sound of my own voice is strangled and strange to my ears.

"I didn't know, really, if you'd want me to call you or not."

She sounds calm. A good sign, I decide. Not the voice of a woman who's calling with terrible news. Unless she's in shock. I've heard people can sound very calm when they're in shock.

"Uh, it's okay," I say. "What —?"

"It's about Devlin."

What's taking her so long? Can't she just tell me — *whatever* it is — get it over with? I say nothing and wait.

"He, well, he asked me to call you, actually."

He asked her … that means he must be alive.

My knees buckle. I sink to the floor in relief. I barely hear what she says next. Only a few words penetrate. Treatment centre.

Something about visitors.

"You can imagine what this means to me," she's saying.

"What did you say the name of the place was?" I blurt. I don't want to hear how happy she is about it. She's the one who put him on the street in the first place. Threw him out for stealing some old jewellery! I remember how she called me back then. I think she expected me to tell her "great job" or something.

"New Valley Treatment Centre," she says.

"Is he allowed visitors?"

"Well, yes, but it's limited. That's why I'm calling. Devlin was hoping you might go to see him. He can have one visitor for a half hour this evening. Supervised. And you have to call first to be put on the list."

"I'll be there," I say. "Thanks."

I can tell that she wants to talk more. She says something about how terrible the past months have been.

"For a lot of people," I say. I wonder if she knows any of the things her son has done for drugs. "Uh, I have to go now. But thanks for letting me know."

She says goodbye reluctantly and hangs up. In seconds I'm on *Canada411*, getting the treatment centre's number. A man answers on the second ring.

"New Valley. This is Bill. What can I do for you?" His voice is rough. I decide he's a heavy smoker.

"I'd like to make an appointment to visit Devlin Mather this evening."

"Devlin, huh? Your name?"

"Lexie Malton."

"You a relative?"

"I'm his girlfriend," I say without thinking. "I mean, I used to be."

"Seven o'clock." Bill sounds bored. "If you're late, you won't get in. If you're high, you won't get in. Personal items have to be locked up. There's no touching or kissing. Visits are half an hour. No exceptions."

"I'll be there," I say. I try to sound responsible — like I'd never think of being late. Or high.

"One other thing," Bill says. "Crying makes it harder for them. So try not to."

"Okay."

My stomach is in knots all afternoon. Oscar phones to see if I want to catch an early movie with Vaughn and Niki. I've already made up my mind to tell him the truth.

"I can't make it tonight. I had a call from Devlin's mother earlier. He's in rehab and she wants me to go talk to him. I said I would."

"He's in rehab?"

"Yes." There's silence for a half a minute or so.

"Well, good," he says. "I hope he gets straightened out."

"So, you don't mind?"

"What, because you used to go out with him?"

"That would bother a lot of guys."

"*Should* I be bothered about it?"

Maybe. Probably.

"No," I say.

"So, don't worry about it." He pauses. "You want me to meet you somewhere after?"

I doubt I'll feel like talking then, but I don't want to say that. "I'll call you," I tell him.

At dinnertime I can hardly eat. It's a bad night for that, too, since Andrea made the meal. She has this very mistaken idea that she's a great cook. Worse, she acts like you're deliberately insulting her if you don't eat what she makes.

I poke at the limp broccoli and dried up baked cod on my plate. I see that Lynne is doing the same. Even Barb, who's the least fussy, isn't eating with any enthusiasm.

"I wish these girls appreciated good, healthy food," Andrea tells Dad. What she *means* is: make your bratty daughters eat.

"Come on now, girls," Dad says. "Andrea puts a lot of work into the meals she makes."

"It's not very good," Barb says. I pretend to cough to cover a smile.

"Now, Barb, honey," Andrea says, "it's not nice to talk that way. You could hurt someone's feelings."

"But it *isn't*," Barb insists. Then she realizes she was being corrected. She claps her hand over her mouth and laughs and says, "Sorry!"

I've passed half of my fish under the table to Kramer while Andrea was looking at Barb. It's the best I'll be able to do. I doubt the existence of an animal that would eat the soggy broccoli. I mush it into the potatoes and try not to gag while I force it down.

It's my turn for dishes. I rush through them, mentally rehearsing things I can say to Devlin. There's barely time to change and put on a touch of makeup.

"I'll be back around eight," I say as I head toward the door. It's a relief, and a bit of good luck, that no one asks where I'm going.

I lose ten minutes waiting to transfer buses and get to New Valley with about three minutes to spare. I'd expected a hospital-like building, so I'm surprised to find myself in front of a big, old-fashioned house.

The door is locked. I guess there's no walking right on in to this place. I stab at the doorbell.

"Yes?"

"I'm, uh, here to see Devlin Mather."

"Your name?"

"Lexie Malton."

A buzzing sound tells me I can go in. A few steps past the door I find a windowed office with a sign over it that says ALL VISITORS MUST SIGN IN. A thirty-ish woman with frizzy blonde hair is inside. She pushes a clipboard with a visitors' sheet on it toward me and says, "Sign here. Then go down the hall, second door on your right. Your first time here, right?"

I nod.

"Put anything you have with you — purse, bag, whatever, into one of the lockers in the hall. Take the key with you and give it to the counsellor on duty when you get to the visiting area."

I do as instructed and then go on to the door to the visiting room. It too, is locked. I knock. Seconds later it's opened by a slim guy who looks to be in his early twenties. He's wearing a T-shirt with Snoopy dancing on his chest.

"I'm Ray Li — a Recovery Worker here at New Valley," he says. He reaches for the key I'm holding. "You must be Lexie."

I try to hide my surprise and hope he can't tell that I thought he was a patient.

"Devlin will be right along," Ray says, waving me toward one of three unmatched couches in the room. "Take a seat. There are a few things we should go over before he gets here."

Then he reviews the things I've already been told. Try not to cry. No touching or kissing. No extensions past half an hour. As he talks, I can tell that he's checking for any signs that I might be high. He never says so, but I see the way he looks at my eyes. He stays in motion too — probably to see how well I follow his movements.

Then the door opens and Devlin comes into the room.

Chapter Ten

Ray ushers Devlin over to a couch at right angles with mine, then takes the third one himself. Devlin sits and stares at his hands. Aside from clean clothes, I can't say he looks a whole lot better than the last time I saw him. The eruptions on his face are scabbed over, but he still looks pale and sickly.

"Hi, Devlin," I say. I'm perilously close to crying, in spite of the warnings.

"Hi." He continues to avoid looking at me.

"I'm really glad you're here," I add.

He nods but the up-and-down motion quickly changes to side-to-side. "I'm sorry about the ring," he says.

"It's okay," I tell him. I remember how I treated him that night. The way I looked at him — like he was dirt. "It doesn't matter."

"And everything else I did," he says.

"No, *I'm* sorry," I say. Tears are coming. I swallow hard and take a deep breath, trying to gulp them back.

He looks over at me. "*You're* sorry?" he echoes. "What've *you* got to be sorry about?"

"Because it was all my fault." I'm crying. I can't help it. "None of this would have happened if it wasn't for me."

"How do you figure that?" He sounds honestly curious.

"Jayden's party," I manage. That's as far as I get. There's silence (aside from my sobbing) for a few moments. I wonder if Devlin is remembering that night. I wonder if he's replaying the moment it all began.

The "quiet room," Jayden called it. He smiled like we were sharing a secret. When the three of us were inside, he locked the door and produced a piece of tinfoil and a packet of white powder.

"Chasing the dragon," he murmured. His eyes were bright. He tapped some powder onto the foil.

"What is that?" Devlin asked.

"This? It's the real deal, my man." Jayden pulled out a lighter and flicked it until a flame rose. "Heroin," he said. The word rolled off his tongue, warm and reverent.

I leaned forward, fascinated and shocked at the same time. It was Devlin who spoke, Devlin who protested. As wasted as he was, it was Devlin who had the sense to voice objections.

"You're worrying about nothing," Jayden

laughed. *"You can't get hooked by smoking it. I'm telling you, man — you gotta try this."*

He held the foil over the flame and, as smoke rose, he drew it into his lungs. It looked so harmless. Inhaling a little smoke. He leaned back, waiting. We were all silent for a moment. His face relaxed into a smile of utter bliss.

I wanted to know how it felt.

"Well, it can't hurt just to try it one time." That was me — drunk and curious and proving I wasn't uptight.

Jayden's smile widened. He prepared some of the white powder for me. Oddly, he pointed out a door at the side of the room.

"Bathroom. Right there," he said. Then the flame flickered and I leaned in as smoke began to rise.

I inhaled, scared but excited, too. It flowed over me slowly, and then, suddenly, I felt an over-powering nausea. I raced to the bathroom, getting to the toilet just in time. My stomach heaved as I vomited, emptying itself into the bowl in splashes of mottled colour.

I didn't care. The drug smoothed it all out — the unpleasantness of puking seemed like nothing. I felt a sort of floating peacefulness.

I smiled at Devlin.

"It's nice," I said, though it was an effort to speak. "Come on, try it."

I'm drawn back to the present by Devlin shaking his head. "Why do you think that was your fault?" he asks.

"Because, I talked you into it. I believed Jayden when he said it wasn't addictive if it was smoked."

"That's one lie we can't seem to kill," Ray says. "You can get hooked on heroin *any* way you use it — but people still think if they aren't cranking, they're safe."

"Cranking?" I repeat.

"Shooting. Needles," Devlin explains. "I was cranking within three weeks of the party at Jayden's place."

I gasp at that, but he nods and says, "It's true. First time I bought direct from a dealer instead of getting it from Jayden. The guy told me the high was faster and better. He gave me some clean works and showed me how to fix."

"Customer service," Ray says with heavy sarcasm.

"Nothing was your fault, Lexie," Devlin tells me. He leans forward, reaches a hand toward me. Mine goes to meet it automatically.

"No touching," Ray reminds us. "Sorry."

We snatch our hands back like they were about to touch fire. "I forgot," I say.

"The no-touching rule will change as Devlin makes progress and earns privileges," Ray says.

After a brief pause he adds, "Recovering addicts have a better chance of success if there's a support network in place for them when they leave here. To that end, we try to build a team of people who will take part in various roles through the recovery process. Devlin would like you to be a member of his team, if you're willing."

"Yes," I say.

"It will mean being here during certain counselling sessions and meetings."

"I have a job," I say. "But I want to help. Can I still do it?"

"You have a job?" Devlin says. "Where?"

"At Subway." I smile as I give him this simple detail of my life. I hope he knows it shows trust, and faith in him.

"We can work around your schedule," Ray tells me. "Devlin still has another week before he gets started on that."

"*Another* week?" I say.

"He's been here for just over two weeks now."

"You've been here for two weeks! Why didn't you let me know before?"

"There are no calls or visitors for the first two weeks," Devlin says. "Anyway, I was pretty sick."

"Oh. Right." I feel foolish for not realizing that. "Was it very bad?"

"Yeah. It was worse than I thought it was going to be. I knew about the puking and the chills and sweating part, but I didn't know how bad it would be. Or how everything — even my bones — would ache like crazy."

"Devlin had a rough time, all right," Ray says. "He barely slept the first week, too, which doesn't help. Withdrawal is never easy — but he's past the worst of the physical stuff."

"It's gotta get better from here on in," Devlin says. He turns slightly, to look directly at me. "I know one thing — I'll never use heroin again. I promise you that."

"I'm so glad." My throat is tight with emotion and my words are barely a whisper. He hears me, though. I hope he hears more than the words.

Chapter Eleven

On the way home on the bus I can hardly sort out what I'm feeling. The one thing I'm sure about is that I *do* want to be with Devlin again. I wish I'd asked how long he'll be at New Valley. We can start to have a normal relationship again as soon as he's out.

I haven't forgotten Oscar. There's no choice but to break up with him. I hate the thought of it. And he doesn't deserve it — he hasn't done anything wrong.

I toy with the idea of waiting a while. After all, Devlin will be in rehab for weeks, maybe months. But I realize that would be worse than telling Oscar the truth now and getting it over with. Worse for the guilt I'd have to carry (and I've done a lot of that lately) and more unfair to him.

The very next afternoon I call him and tell him I'm coming by.

"I need to talk to you," I say, hoping he'll hear the hidden message in those words. I'm not sure whether guys get that sort of thing, though, so I don't know what to expect when I get there.

It looks like he got it, all right. When I make it to his place, he lets me in without a hug or a kiss, and his smile is forced.

We walk silently into the living room and I sit on the couch. Oscar takes the chair across the room, facing me. He waits for me to speak.

"I, uh," I start, then pause and clear my throat. My mouth is dry. "Could I have a glass of water?" I ask.

"Sure." He disappears into the kitchen. I fight the urge to get up and bolt while he's out of the room.

"Thanks," I say, as he returns and passes me the glass. When he's back in his chair, I try again. "Look, Oscar, you're a great guy. And I really mean that."

He says nothing. I feel slightly irritated by his calm, quiet manner. I *know* he knows what's coming. He *could* help me out a bit by saying something to move it along.

"I need to talk about ... us."

"So, talk."

"I, uh, the thing is, it's just not there for me. I like you — a lot, but not the way I should."

"Not the way you like Devlin," he says. "Or do you want me to think it's a coincidence that you saw him last night and you're here breaking up with me today?"

"It's not the way you make it sound," I say. "It's that Devlin needs me right now. And honestly, I never would have broken up with him in the first place if he hadn't got, you know, hooked."

"So, you're breaking up with me to go back out with a junkie," Oscar says. His voice is matter-of-fact, but his eyes give him away. There's hurt behind his composed front.

"He's in rehab," I say. "And he swears he'll never use again."

"I hope he doesn't," Oscar tells me. "I've got nothing against the guy. But I thought things were going pretty good with us."

"They were," I say. "I didn't mean for this to happen."

He says nothing for a few long moments. I search my head for words to make this less painful, but there are none. The urge to cross the room and put my arms around him is strong at one point, but I don't. I know he'll see it as pity (which it isn't) and that will only make him feel worse.

Finally, when I feel that I can't take another second of silence, he speaks.

"I think you're making a mistake," he says. "I mean, do what you have to do — I'm not telling you this to try to keep things going with us, that's over no matter what — but be careful."

The caring in his words gets to me more than anything else he might have said. I need to get out of there before I break down and cry.

"I'm *really* sorry, Oscar," I say. And then I go. I pause at the door, but there's nothing to say.

It turns out that it's easier to tell Oscar than it is to tell some other people — once it's official, that is. On my second visit to New Valley, I tell Devlin that I've broken up with Oscar. He asks, in a broken voice, if he has a chance to get me back.

"You *have* me back," I say and his eyes fill with tears. "I'll be here for you all the way. I know you're going to make it."

His face is earnest as he vows, "I *am* going to make it, Lexie."

I'm glad, so glad, that he's committed to staying straight. But I know not everyone is going to have the faith I have, or be thrilled to know I'm back with him.

Dori, of course, is true blue to the end. She's one of the few people who get behind the whole idea.

"I always thought you and Dev were so good together," she tells me with shining eyes. "And now you two are going to have a happy ending after all."

My father is definitely less enthused.

"Have you lost your mind?" he wants to know. Standing beside him, Andrea can't seem to decide whether to look disapproving or concerned. Or maybe she's constipated, who knows? I somehow manage to keep from telling her to pick a face and stick with it.

"He's clean now, Dad," I say. "And he's going to stay that way."

"Look, Lexie, it's not that I didn't like Devlin. You know he's been here many times — I thought he was a nice enough kid. But he's a *heroin* addict. He'd have to prove himself for a good long time before I'd ever feel comfortable letting you go out with him."

"So, he'll do that. Prove himself, I mean," I say. "We can see each other *here* if we have to. But I'm not going to turn my back on him now. I can't, and you can't ask me to."

"I don't want you with him unsupervised until I'm fully, one hundred percent satisfied that it's safe for you," Dad says. "Do you give me your word?"

"Yes, sure," I say, too relieved to argue. I'm surprised he's not taking a harder line.

"No exceptions. When he gets out of rehab, the only way you'll see him will be in this house, with either myself or Andrea home. Clear?"

"Yes, Dad, it's clear!" I say, trying not to sound annoyed. I feel like I'm being treated like a baby, but I know better than to push it. At least, not for a while.

Anyway, I'm sure that once he sees how great Devlin is doing, he'll loosen up.

Chapter Twelve

I see Devlin four times over the next week. Things are going great. He looks better and better. For one thing, a volunteer hairdresser who comes to the treatment centre once a month has given him a hot new haircut. What's more, the colour is coming back to his skin and he's starting to smile. Like the old Dev.

I feel happier than I've been in so long. It sits in me, like a joyous song in my heart. I know that sounds lame, but it's the best I can do to describe it.

I'm off work on Monday and I have time to kill before I go to New Valley for a visit. My stomach is a madhouse of flutters! Today, Devlin will have moved up a step. For the first time since we've been back together, we'll be able to hold hands.

That probably sounds silly, but it's been torturous, not being able to touch him.

Dori comes over for lunch. I've told her the basics of what's happened, but we haven't really had a chance to talk.

"I always thought Devlin was the one you really cared for," she says. "And I knew, if anything would bring him back, it would be you."

I smile. "It's been hard, though, Dori. When he was using, it was so awful, because he wasn't there anymore. His personality just vanished."

"I don't know what I'd do if anything like this ever happened to A.J.," she says with a shudder. "He's no doper, though, so I think I'm safe. I hope I'd be as strong as you've been — not that I ever want to find out. "

I don't like the doper comment and the way it implies Devlin *was* one, which he wasn't. Not before the heroin. I'm on the verge of telling her the whole truth, but shame keeps me quiet.

I've never talked to anyone besides Devlin about Jayden's party, except at New Valley. I remember waking the next morning, feeling horrible and stunned to remember what had happened the night before. It's not something I would *ever* have done if I hadn't been drinking.

I draw myself back to what Dori is saying and realize she's asking me about Oscar.

"So, what did he say when you broke up with him?" she asks.

"Oh, Oscar." I look down at my hands sadly. "It was awful, telling him. He was pretty decent about it, but I know it hurt him."

"Poor guy," Dori says. "And poor Jen."

"Jen?"

"Jen Fahey. I ran into her at the Brentwood Mall on Saturday. She was all excited because she and Oscar started going out a couple of days ago. Obviously, it's a rebound thing."

"Oh," I say. "Right." I force a smile onto my face. Ridiculous as it is, I feel a bit miffed at the thought that Oscar is already seeing some-one else. I tell myself I'm glad, but, really, it's kind of insulting to be replaced that fast!

Of course, that's silly. And unimportant. What matters is that Devlin is clean and we're back together. Kind of a fairy-tale ending.

By the time I get to New Valley, I've decided I'm happy about Oscar and Jen. After all, I have Devlin and that's what matters.

When I get to New Valley at 7:00 I'm nearly sick with excitement, but also shy in a strange kind of way. He is, too; I can see it in his face when he's ushered into the room.

I'm standing near the window — sitting is impossible when you're all nerved up that way. He crosses to me, stands there for a second or two and then reaches out a hand and touches my face.

"I've been thinking about how soft your skin is," he says.

Ray is on duty today and he turns his head to the side. I know he can still see us in his peripheral vision, but it's better than having someone stare straight at you.

Devlin's hand drops, takes hold of mine, and he draws me to the couch. We sit together and the visit slips by in what seems like seconds. I can hardly remember a thing we talked about afterward, but the pressure of his hand, gently squeezing mine, remains with me for hours.

Chapter Thirteen

It's all routine by now. Getting buzzed in, locking up my stuff, being eyeballed for any sign of drug use.

I'm a bit early today, which won't do me any good. It's not like they'll start the visit before 7:00. I'll just end up sitting on a bench beside the lockers, waiting, but I don't mind. It gives me a good feeling, just thinking about the fact that Devlin is in the building, and knowing that he'll soon appear and his face will light up with a smile when he sees me. Best of all, he's moved up another step on the privilege scale. The last two visits he's been allowed to actually hug me and I can hardly wait.

I go straight to the reception window as soon as I'm inside. There's a guy there who I haven't seen before.

"I'm Lexie," I say, though he already knows that since he just buzzed me in. "Signing in for Devlin."

"I tried to call you earlier," he says.

"My phone was charging." My heart sinks a little. "Did Devlin do something to lose his visit tonight?" The rules at this place can be pretty crazy. You do the least little thing wrong and there goes a privilege.

"I'm sorry, but Devlin left."

"Left?" He might as well have punched me in the gut. "What do you mean — he *left*?"

"He decided not to finish the program."

"Where did he *go*?"

"I don't know."

"Maybe he went home," I say. My heart is pounding with fear.

"It's possible, but when we called his mother she didn't seem to be aware of any plan for him to go there."

"So, maybe he just decided — he can be impulsive," I say. "He might have felt ready to handle it out of here. There are so many *rules* in here."

The guy looks at me sadly. I can see that he's heard this lots before. People grasping at hope, trying to convince themselves that things will be okay.

The sidewalk blurs as I make my way back to the bus stop. I pull my phone out and dial Devlin's house. Even as I punch in the numbers, I know he's not going to be there.

"Hello?" Mrs. Mather's voice is both strained and eager. I realize at once that she's hoping the call is from Devlin.

"It's Lexie," I say.

"Oh." No attempt to hide her disappointment.

"I just found out that Devlin left New Valley."

She starts to sob and the sound makes me cry, too. It's the first time we've agreed on anything since she sent Devlin to the street. When she gets herself under control enough to talk, she moans out, "I don't know what to do."

I don't know, either. "Is there anywhere else he might have gone?" I ask.

"Like where?"

"A relative's place maybe?"

"That doesn't make any sense, Lexie. Why would he go to a relative's house instead of his own home?"

"He might not be sure he *can* come home," I say. I think, but don't add, *since you threw him out before*.

She starts to cry again. I guess she got the message, anyway. "Of course he can come home — if he's not using," she blubbers. "Do you think he's already taken something?"

I ask myself, is there *any* faint hope that Devlin left New Valley for any other reason than to score and get high?

"Probably," I say. "Unless he hasn't been able to get any."

"Maybe he hasn't!" she says. "He didn't have any money. If we could find him in time, we might be able to talk him into going back to the treatment centre."

It's a thin hope, but somehow I buy in. Ten minutes later she's pulling up at the stop and I'm getting into her car.

For the next few hours we drive up and down the streets surrounding Main and Hastings. Devlin is most likely to be in that area, but I know there are other places, as well. If he managed to get his hands on some cash, he'll be out of sight somewhere. We could be driving right past him and never know it.

There are lots of people around — most of them in their twenties, a few older and some teens. They're in doorways and alleys and leaning against buildings. Some are moving aimlessly along the street. Others have that quick and nervous "gotta score" twitch in their step.

Most ignore us. Those who pay any attention at all watch us with a sort of detached interest. I suppose they're used to seeing desperate family members searching for loved ones.

"Maybe we should ask a few people if they've seen him," Mrs. Mather suggests.

"No one here is going to help us," I tell her.

"I have a picture of him in my wallet," she says next. "What if we show it around and offer a reward if anyone can tell us where he is?"

"In that case," I say with a sigh, "*everyone* will know where he is. Except nothing they tell you will be true."

She knows I'm right. She doesn't argue, but tears slide down her cheeks.

"I've never known what to do about this, Lexie," she tells me.

It's probably the closest she's ever come to wondering if she made a mistake by putting Devlin out of the house. But then, I've enabled him, taking him money, so who am I to judge her? At least she wasn't helping him get high.

"I don't think it matters that much," I say. "There isn't a whole lot anyone can do until he's ready to get clean."

"I thought this was it," she whispers.

"So did I. So did Devlin, I think. At least he made a start. We just have to believe he'll come around again, and be there for him when he does."

"I'm so afraid," she says, barely loud enough for me to hear.

I don't answer. I don't want to hear about her fears. It's all I've been able to do to keep mine from crowding in on me. Too many terrible endings are possible. Devlin, wasting away, month by month, year by year — disappearing more and more into this world of the living dead. Devlin, dead from an overdose, or AIDS. Devlin, brain damaged from a bad dose or a beating.

Thankfully, I'm drawn from these thoughts when a familiar-looking figure appears from around a corner ahead.

"Is that *him*?"

A bright burst of hope, quickly gone when we draw closer and see that it isn't Devlin. The disappointment is bitter and every moment that ticks by erodes what hope remains.

We give up a little while before midnight. When Devlin's mother drops me off at my place we're both too exhausted to speak. I get out of the car and go into the house without looking back.

Chapter Fourteen

I know he'll call. He'll call and tell me what happened and why he left New Valley. We'll talk and, even though he's using again, it will be different. This time he'll listen, because now he wants help. If he didn't, he wouldn't have gone for treatment in the first place.

I know he'll never call. He was clean, we were back together — he had every reason in the world to stay off it. And he made a choice. He chose to live in filth on the street. He chose to go back to getting into cars with men. He picked heroin over his family and his girlfriend — over his life. He picked heroin over everything.

I go back and forth constantly. It will come out okay. It will never be okay.

I cling to some of the things he said in meetings. Like the reasons he *swore* he would never go back to the street.

"You know that first high?" he asked. "The rush that goes through you?"

"But you got so sick," I pointed out. "Way worse than I did. You threw up, like, four times."

"Didn't matter," he told me. "I still wanted that feeling again. But I never got it."

I guess I looked as surprised as I felt to hear that. He explained.

"You never get that first-time feeling back," he said. "You just keep chasing it. And then, after a while, you realize you really aren't getting high at all. Once you're hooked and you use for a while, you need it just to feel normal, to walk around with your head up and to be able to talk to people. You're empty and numb and the only thing you care about is your next fix."

I try not to picture the look on Devlin's face when he talked about that first time. I try not to think about the fact that he didn't want to do it — wasn't going to do it, until I persuaded him.

I call New Valley the fourth day after Devlin left, and ask to speak to Ray Li. I'm not even sure, as I dial, why I'm calling. I just need to talk to someone.

"It's Lexie," I say when he comes to the phone. "I just wondered if maybe anyone there had heard from Devlin. And since you worked with him a lot, I figured you'd know."

"Sorry," Ray tells me, "but he hasn't called."

"People who leave the way Devlin did — do they ever come back right away?"

"It happens, sure. But it's been, what, three, four days now?"

"Four," I say. "Is that bad?"

"Leaving at all is bad, but now and then someone will call within a day or two. Sometimes they haven't even used and they come back. Or, if they have used, it's a one-, maybe two-time thing, and they get right back into the program."

Ray pauses. I wait without speaking. I know there's more coming.

"Once they're out for any longer than that, it's usually because they've slipped right back into their old pattern of using. And honestly, using even once is really dangerous when someone is off the stuff for a while."

"Like, for an overdose?" I ask, even though I'm afraid of the answer.

"There's always a danger of overdose," Ray says. "Some of the stuff out there is pretty pure and no one knows exactly what they're getting when they score. There have been cases, too, of kids smoking it off the wrong surface and dying, or being severely brain damaged. None of it is really safe. But that's not actually what I meant.

"What I did mean, is that, when an addict is off heroin for a while and uses again, it gives them the kind of high that got them hooked in the first place. You heard Devlin describe how using gets to be something to keep from going into withdrawal. But after they're clean, they get the high back — the rush. For a while, anyway. And because of that, it's really easy for them to sink back into full-blown use again."

"I was thinking, if I could find him, maybe I could get him to come back," I say. "Do you have any suggestions? Like, things I could say to him that might work?"

"Honestly, Lexie, my best advice to you is to stay as far away from Devlin as you can. Until he decides on his own to get back into treatment, there really isn't anything you can say or do."

"I just want to help," I say.

"I get that. But you're far more likely to end up getting hurt. It's kind of like standing on a chair and trying to pull someone who's standing on the floor up. They'll drag you down a lot faster than you'll pull them up onto it."

"There's one other thing I've been wondering. A lot," I tell Ray.

"Okay," he prompts.

"Why didn't I get hooked, too? We both tried it the same way at the same time. How come Devlin ended up addicted and I never touched it again?"

"Did you ever think about doing it again?"

"I dunno. I guess not. Not seriously, anyway."

"That's the thing with heroin. You don't know who's going to get hooked and who isn't. But very few people can use it recreationally. You're one of the lucky ones — it didn't grab you right away. If you'd kept dabbling with it, believe me, it wouldn't have taken long before you'd have been addicted, too."

He pauses. Maybe he can hear in my silence that he hasn't really answered my question.

"But as far as, why him, why not you? Nobody knows."

"Have you ever tried it?"

"Nope."

That surprises me. For some reason, I had the idea that a lot of drug counsellors are former addicts themselves. "You were never curious?" I ask.

He laughs, but there's no humour in it. "Sure," he says, "but there's curious smart and curious dumb. I like to stay in the first group. If there was a bottle of a hundred pills sitting on the table in front of you, and I told you, half of these are safe and half are deadly poison — certain death, would you take one?"

"Of course not," I say.

"Well, that's the kind of risk people take every day with heroin," he says. "Because they're *curious*!"

Chapter Fifteen

I don't go looking for Devlin. Turns out, I don't have to.

It's just a little over a week later and I'm at work, making a sub for one of our regular customers. I happen to glance up and there he is, standing on the sidewalk outside. He's watching through the plate glass that forms a large part of the outside walls. When he sees me looking at him, he lifts a hand, gives a weak wave, and tries to smile.

I'm horrified as he starts to move toward the door. I picture him coming in and demanding money, making a scene.

"Uh, I have to step outside just for a minute," I tell Paula, my co-worker. She starts to object, but I'm already past her and halfway to the door. "I'll be right back," I say over my shoulder.

Devlin looks bad, like he hasn't slept in days. He reaches for my hand. I let him take it.

"I'm sorry, babe," he says.

"I'm not giving you any money," I tell him.

"I know I let you down," he says, like he didn't hear me, "but I'm going to get back on track, I swear."

"You're going back to New Valley?" I ask.

"Yeah, of course," he says.

"When?"

"I just need to get smoothed out first," he tells me.

I look straight at him. I want to believe him, but I know the way his hands are fidgeting means he needs a fix. And that means he'll say anything.

"I swear, Lexie," he says softly. "If you give me a few bucks, that's all I need. I just need to get myself levelled out. Then I can handle the first night there. You know, get some rest to face coming off it tomorrow."

"I don't have any money on me," I say.

"Yeah, but, where's your purse?"

"I don't bring my purse to work," I lie.

"Well, just get me ten bucks from the cash register," he says. The pleading has left his voice. It's gone hard and determined.

"I'm not stealing money so you can get high," I say. I'm angry with myself for listening to him. Everything he just told me is a lie and I know it. He has no intention of going back to New Valley tonight. All he wants is money for heroin.

"Ten bucks!" he yells, in an instant rage. "I'm asking for ten lousy bucks!"

"I'm not giving you money," I say.

And then it happens. It's so fast I hardly register what's taking place at first. He grabs my arm and turns me around so that he's behind me. I feel myself being pushed forward. I nearly stumble as my feet are propelled along the sidewalk.

"What are you doing? Let go of me!" I say. I'm angry, but I'm not scared. Not yet.

"You're going to help me get some money," he says.

"I am not!"

We've passed the front of the Subway shop. I wonder what Paula is thinking. Probably that I'm being a big, irresponsible jerk leaving her to handle all the work. Anyone watching most likely just sees a guy and girl hurrying along.

It's beginning to dawn on me that he really means business. That this could be bad. I remember, in sessions at New Valley, how he described the craving.

"*Nothing matters then except getting a fix. You don't care about anyone or anything.*"

"Okay, okay," I say. "Let go of me. I'll get you some money."

He laughs. It's a harsh, scornful sound. He wants me to know that he's not fooled as easily as I was. The funny thing is, I'm telling the truth.

"I mean it," I say. "You can even come in with me. I'll get you some money. I'll get you twenty."

"You had your chance," he says. "You think I'm stupid?"

"Well, how am I supposed to get you money if you won't let me get my purse?"

"You just told me you don't have your purse with you."

"I'm sorry, Dev, honestly. I didn't realize you were in such bad shape. But now I do, and I want to help."

He wrenches my arm, twisting it up behind me. I yelp in pain. He relaxes it just enough for it to stop hurting.

"Shut up," he says. "Now, you just do what I tell you and this will be over in no time."

"What? What will be over?" I can hardly breathe for the panic in my chest.

Devlin doesn't answer. Instead, he applies pressure to my arm again, forcing me up on tiptoe.

"Okay, okay. I'm sorry," I say. I don't even know why the question made him angry. I decide I'd better stay quiet.

There's a small convenience store on the corner. He steers me toward the door and that's when I know. He's going to rob the place. I wonder why he's brought me along. Clearly, the craving is preventing him from thinking straight.

I feel myself shoved through the door, Devlin still right on my back and holding my arm. We're barely inside when he leans forward and murmurs, "Just go along with this and everything will be okay."

"Come on, Devlin, don't do this," I say.

"Oh, we're doing it," he tells me. He smiles but it's grim and ghastly and completely without mirth. He leans down and kisses my cheek.

I realize that he's let go of my arm. Rubbing my shoulder, I turn toward him. I have to try to talk him out of this.

That's when I see the knife in his hand.

Chapter Sixteen

It's funny how your brain works. Even though I have plenty of proof that what's happening is real, my first thought is: "He's just messing with me."

Shock, I guess. Refusal to believe something terrible is true. Whatever it is, it doesn't last long.

"Turn around," he says. His voice is low and menacing.

"Devlin, please," I stammer.

"Turn around," he repeats. Fury is rising in his face. I obey.

"Walk to the cash," he says.

I move forward as slowly as I can. Trying to think. Trying to buy time. There's a chubby woman at the cash — probably in her fifties. She looks up, sees me. It registers on her face. She knows at once that something is wrong.

"Yes?" she says. She's trying to sound normal.

Devlin moves suddenly. He presses up against me and circles my waist with his left arm. His right hand moves up, bringing the blade of the knife to my throat.

"Give me the money in the cash," he tells her, "unless you want to see a *lot* of blood."

Her hand goes to her mouth and her eyes widen, but she doesn't make a sound.

"Now!" Devlin yells.

The blade is cold and sharp against my skin.

"Hurry up!" he yells, jerking with the effort.

A sliver of pain registers, like the sting of a paper cut.

"Devlin," I say, fighting to stay calm, "please be careful. You're cutting me."

He leans around to check and relaxes the knife. As he does this, the woman at the cash reaches under the counter. I'm stunned when she produces a gun. She holds it up, wild-eyed, and points it at me. Or, I suppose, at *us*, really, since Devlin is squarely behind me.

"Get out," she says. "Get out or I'll shoot."

"You gonna shoot a hostage?" Devlin sneers.

"Hostage *nothing*," she answers. The gun in her hand has made her brave. "You two are in on this together."

"No!" I say. I can't take my eyes off the gun in her hand. "It's not that way — I swear."

"Sure it's not," she says. Her voice doesn't waver.

And then I feel myself moving again — closer now. I'm right up against the counter. The knife has moved away from my throat and is pointing at the woman. The gun trembles in her hand.

"Back up," she yells. "I'll shoot."

"No! *Please*," I beg.

Then there's a flash of movement and the knife appears like magic, sticking into her shoulder. She screams and drops the gun. As she grabs the knife handle and pulls it out, Devlin is up and over the counter. He bends and when he straightens up, the gun is in his hand.

"Give me the knife," he says, holding his free hand out. "Nice and easy."

She drops it into his open palm. Her whole body is vibrating. "Please," she whimpers, "please don't shoot me."

"Then give me the money. RIGHT NOW!" Devlin orders.

Blood is oozing from the wound in her shoulder. A dark red trail makes its way down the pale green sweater she's wearing. She's shaking so hard that she can barely control her hand to punch keys on the cash register. She stabs jerkily at a few buttons, but nothing happens.

I wonder — if I turn and run, will he let me go? I tell myself that it's Devlin, that there's no way he'd shoot me. But my feet won't move.

Devlin shoves the gun into the woman's side. "Stop jerking me around!" he shouts at her.

"I'm trying," she says. She's crying and shaking and bleeding. There's blood running down her sleeve now, making three or four trails across her hand. The cash register is smudged with red from her attempts to open it.

I try to think. Can I get the gun away from him? His finger is on the trigger and he seems to be holding it good and tight. And it's pointed at the woman. I can't take a chance.

She's totally falling apart now, sobbing and blubbering out words that make no sense. I think I hear her say something about having children.

"Shut up!" Devlin yells.

She can't seem to stop herself. The jumble of words keeps on coming while she pushes at buttons on the register. And then, suddenly, it dings and slides open.

Devlin shoves her aside. She bangs into a display case behind her and sinks down, sliding to the floor. He reaches into the cash register and begins to pull out bills. He shoves them into his pockets with one hand while the other continues to clutch the gun.

I see the woman eyeing the gun and hope she won't try anything. It's clear that she's still very frightened, but she's beginning to calm down. Very slowly, she begins to get back to her feet. Her eyes never leave Devlin. He, on the other hand, seems unaware of anything except the money.

I clear my throat, willing her to look at me. If only she'd glance my way, maybe I could get a message across. I don't like the way she keeps staring at the gun.

I wish I could tell her that there's no need for her to try anything at this point in the game. Surely she doesn't think he might shoot her now. After all, he has what he wants.

She's inching toward him. I open my mouth to say something — anything — to stop her. But it's too late.

She lunges at the gun.

Devlin spins and jerks his arm.

And there's another sound. A bell tinkling.

The door opens.

A little Chinese girl — maybe twelve years old, walks in.

And then, the roaring CRACK that I will hear for the rest of my life.

The sound of a gun firing.

Chapter Seventeen

I'm bent over her when the emergency services start to arrive. Her eyes are closed and her face shows no sign of pain, only surprise. There's not too much blood. I tell myself that's a good sign, but she's so small, maybe she doesn't have a lot in her to begin with. I can hear a slight rattle as she breathes.

The police get there first. They're gentle and kind when they tell me I have to move. One of them takes my place, bent over the little girl. Unlike me, the officer knows what to do and I watch as she checks for vital signs.

The ambulance arrives next, followed by a second squad car, and then a third and fourth. The officer who moved into my spot over the girl yields to a paramedic. I study his grim face for a moment and then move to a corner to wait.

Devlin is gone. The shot was still echoing when he bolted for the door, jumping over the Chinese girl on the way. I wonder if he's scored yet, if he's leaning back against a wall somewhere with a needle plunged into a vein.

An officer comes to my corner. He tells me I'm a witness and I need to give a statement. He leads me to a car and has me sit in the back seat.

There are so many questions. He starts with my name and date of birth. He writes his questions and my answers on pages on a clipboard.

"Were you already in the store when the shooter came in?"

"I went in just before him," I tell him.

"And where were you when he approached the cash?"

"I was ahead of him. I mean, he was walking right behind me the whole time."

"Did you see him pull out the gun?"

"Devlin didn't have the gun at first — the cashier got that from under the counter," I explain. "He pulled out a knife, and held it to my throat and told the cashier to give him money or there was going to be blood all over the place. Something like that."

"Devlin," repeats the cop. His voice is different — less gentle. "Did you know this person?"

"Yeah. Devlin Mather. He, uh, he used to be my boyfriend."

"I see." He doesn't sound like he sees. "And when did you and, Devlin, break up?"

"We broke up a long time ago," I say. "And then we started to go out again just a little while ago. I guess we didn't 'officially' break up this time. It's a bit complicated."

"Okay," he says. There's a pause. I feel like I need to explain, but I'm trying to see what's going on inside the store at the same time and it's hard to sort out what I should say.

The ambulance workers are finally lifting the stretcher. She's so tiny that it almost looks like there's no one on it. My stomach clenches, watching them carry this limp little girl who a few short moments ago was innocently on her way to the store.

I try to tell the officer that I feel like I'm going to throw up, but my mouth is so dry that I can't speak. Then he gets out of the car. He says he'll be back in a moment.

Someone starts to moan, "noooo," over and over again, like that might change what's just happened. I realize the sounds are coming from me.

It startles me when the officer comes back. He clears his throat.

"I'm going to take you downtown, to the station," he says. "We'll finish up the interview there."

The drive there is a blank, like it never happened. I wonder if I talked with the officer on the way there. When we get to the station, they take me to a room with a table and leave me alone for a while.

It's a different officer who comes in later. He's followed by a female cop. They sit down at the table. He sits across from me and she takes a chair at the end.

"I'm Officer Campbell and this is Officer Neally," the male cop says. "Before we get started, would you like something to drink?"

"Water, please," I say.

Officer Campbell leaves and comes back with a Styrofoam cup of water. I want to gulp it all at once, but I force myself to take tiny sips.

"The first thing we need to know — and we need you to be truthful with us," Officer Neally says, "is where we can find Devlin."

"I don't know. I haven't seen him for weeks."

That earns me some raised eyebrows.

"Until today, that is," I add hastily.

"Do you think we're stupid?" Officer Campbell asks.

"No, of course not."

He leans forward, like we're sharing secrets. "Look, Lexie, the best thing you can do for yourself is level with us right here and now. We know you were in on this. So far, you're just an accomplice. Things don't have to be as hard on you. But the sooner you start being honest with us, the better. Otherwise, it's going to get a lot worse."

"You think Devlin won't give you up if he can make a deal for himself?" asks Neally before

I have time to absorb what Officer Campbell has just said.

"We can't help you if you lie to us," Campbell throws in.

"I *am* telling you the truth," I say. "I was working — I have a job at Subway, and he went there and forced me to go with him."

"So, there will be people — co-workers, customers — at Subway who can back this up? Devlin coming in there and *forcing* you to leave with him? It must have caused quite a ruckus."

I feel confused. "He, well, he didn't come inside, exactly. He was going to — he was walking toward the door. So, I went out — to keep him from coming in and causing trouble."

"Well, wasn't that thoughtful," Officer Neally says. Her voice is thick with sarcasm. "And after you happened to go outside to meet him, he just happened to decide to rob a store a few doors away from where you work. With your help."

"I *wasn't* helping him," I say. "He had a *knife* — he held it to my throat!"

The cops exchange a look. I can't quite read it but I can see there's a message there between them. One thing is clear — they're not all that interested in what I have to say. Something has already convinced them that I'm guilty. And every time I open my mouth, I'm somehow managing to make things worse.

"Please, can someone call my father?" I say. "I don't want to say anything else until he gets me a lawyer."

They go into an act then, like they *tried* to help me, but I just wouldn't let them. Neally shakes her head and shrugs. Campbell throws his hands up. One of them mumbles something about innocent people not needing lawyers.

I don't bite. I figure I've done myself enough harm already.

I'm left alone again. Tears come. I can't stop them.

Chapter Eighteen

The lawyer arrives even before my dad gets there. I've just pulled myself together when the interview door opens suddenly and he comes in, smiling. He offers his free hand while the other clutches a leather briefcase.

"Miss Malton? My name is Karan Paralkar," he says. "I'll be representing you in this matter."

This matter? It sounds small and unimportant, like the whole thing is nothing.

"You're a lawyer?" I ask, even though the answer is obvious.

He smiles. "Don't I look like one?" he asks. I wonder if answering a question with another question is something lawyers do automatically.

"Uh, sure, but my dad has a lawyer," I say. "I was kind of expecting her."

"Yes, Ms. Aballard," he says. "Actually, she's the one who referred your father to me. Her area is family law and you need someone who works in criminal law. That's my field."

"But, I'm not a criminal."

"All the more reason for you to have a criminal lawyer in a situation like this," he tells me. I must look puzzled or doubtful or something because he adds, "Just trust me, okay?"

"Okay," I say. Then, all of a sudden, tears are coming again. I feel foolish, crying in front of a stranger, but I can't stop.

"I know it must be overwhelming," he says when I've managed to swallow back the sobs, "but you'll get through it. Just try to relax and take it one thing at a time."

His advice instantly reminds me of one of the beliefs they talk about at the centre, breaking it down, staying clean by getting through a day or an hour or even a minute at a time. Whatever you can handle without using.

I'm thinking about this, and the hope that was alive in that place, when Dad comes in. He looks scared as he crosses the room and scoops me up out of my seat and into a hug.

This time I don't even try to keep from crying. I'm clinging to my father like his arms are the only safe place in the world and he's patting my back and saying that it's okay. The problem is, that's not true and he knows it as well as I do. I can tell by the way his voice trembles and cracks.

Behind us, the lawyer has risen to his feet. He moves forward once I've forced myself to let go of Dad and step back.

"Karan Paralkar," he says, shaking Dad's hand. "I just got here a few minutes ago so I haven't had much of a chance to talk to Lexie yet."

"Just as well," Dad says. "I'd like to hear what happened myself. Lexie wasn't exactly clear when she called. Just said she'd been arrested for a robbery and shooting."

"Lexie hasn't actually been arrested," Karan informs us, "though it's easy to see why she thought she had. The truth is, she's been free to leave anytime she wanted to this whole time."

I'm on my feet in a flash. "I can *go?*"

"You can, but at this point there's no sense in it. The police are going to proceed with charges, so we might as well wait and deal with it. It will be better than having them pull up to your house and haul you out in handcuffs."

Just the thought of that happening makes my throat tighten. Dad looks away from me, and down at his hands.

"Mr. Paralkar —" I say, but he cuts me off, telling me to call him Karan.

"I swear, I had nothing to do with any of it, Karan," I say.

"Okay," he answers, like that's not really important.

"I tried to explain it to them," I tell him. "But they kept twisting everything I said, until it sounded like I was involved. I swear I *wasn't.*"

"Lexie has never been in any kind of trouble," Dad adds.

"That's good. That will work in her favour," Karan says. "And, Lexie, you'll have a chance to tell me all about what happened, but right now, the first order of business is to find out what the charges are going to be. Give me a couple of minutes and I'll be back."

It's hard, but I turn to face Dad once Karan is gone. His face starts to crumble and he takes a couple of deep breaths. "I don't understand *why* you were *with* that ... that *druggie*, when this all happened," he says.

"He came to my work, Dad. I saw him there and I didn't want him to come in and cause trouble, so I went outside to talk to him for a minute. Then he made me go with him to the store."

"I didn't want you having anything to do with him," Dad says.

"I know. I know that, Dad. And you were right, but I never thought Devlin would do something like this."

"You can't trust an addict," Dad says. "That's what Andrea and I tried to tell you."

"Could you leave her out of this?" I know that's the wrong thing to say, even as the words come out of my mouth.

"Did it ever once occur to you that Andrea

might have your best interests at heart?" he says angrily.

No. It never did. Quite the opposite, in fact. But I don't say so. Why make it worse than it already is?

"Sorry," I say, instead. "I'm just so scared."

"Fine. But don't take it out on Andrea. She does her best by you girls."

I'm saved from having to hear more of that just then. Karan comes back into the room and slides into a seat opposite me. He looks grim.

"I'm afraid you're not going home tonight," he says. "I've asked for a bail hearing as soon as possible, so, with any luck, we'll be able to get you out within a day or two. In the meantime, you're being remanded to Burnaby Youth Custody Services."

He pauses and lets that news sink in. I can't speak. Dad looks like he has questions but can't get them out.

"What happens in these cases generally depends on the seriousness of the charge," Karan explains. He's speaking slowly, choosing his words carefully. "I'm afraid this one is about as bad as it gets."

He pauses, glances from me to my dad and back. A cold feeling is crawling over me and I know what his next words will be before he says them.

"The shooting victim didn't make it. She died less than an hour after they got her to the hospital, so what we're now dealing with is homicide."

Chapter Nineteen

The next thing I know, I'm in the sheriff's van. As we get close to Burnaby, the shock of my situation begins to wear off. My thoughts clear and come into focus. Now, the only thing I can think about is the little girl. Her face, smiling, coming through the doorway of the store. I wonder what she was there to buy. Chewing gum? A treat of some sort? Or perhaps she was sent on an errand for her mother. Maybe milk was needed, or eggs, or some other everyday item.

She woke up this morning like any other day, and went through the day doing normal things. She might have made a few phone calls, watched a little television. Maybe she laughed, or cried, or had an argument with a parent or sister or someone. She didn't feel anything different in the air around her, anything that would tell her it was the final day of her life.

When she walked to the store, she had no idea that she was taking the last steps she would ever take.

She didn't do anything wrong. All she did was open a door and walk inside a store. She walked in at the exact second in time that would mean the end of her life. One minute either way might have been safe. If she'd met with a friend on the street and talked for a moment, that might have saved her. Or, maybe she *did* bump into a friend, or stopped to tie her shoe, or met some other small delay, and it was just long enough to prevent her from entering that brief bit of time earlier that could have saved her life.

She walked in without any thought that she was stepping into the precise spot that she had to be standing in for the bullet to steal her life. Two inches to the left or right might have made all the difference in the world.

Who knows how many things came together for her to be right there, right at that exact second in time? And then a bullet met her and the light was gone out of her eyes forever.

A voice breaks through my thoughts. It's the sheriff, wanting to know where I go to school. I stare at him, not quite able to understand the question at first. It somehow seems like the strangest thing in the world he could have said to me, just because it's so normal.

"Killarney," I tell him once it sinks in.

"Uh, huh? What grade are you in?"

I want to scream at him, to tell him not to ask stupid questions about things that don't matter. Instead, I say, "I don't want to be rude, but I really don't feel like talking right now."

"Perfectly understandable," he says.

There's a woman in the passenger seat. She's wearing a uniform like his so I figure she's some kind of deputy. She turns to me now and asks if I'm nervous.

"Sure she is," the sheriff answers for me. "It's her first time."

"At least Burnaby isn't too far for your family to visit," says the woman. "And Burnaby Youth Custody Services Centre is a nice facility. Besides, you'll be surprised how fast you'll get used to it."

I shove down the urge to yell that I will *not* get used to it, that I didn't *do* anything, and I shouldn't be going there *at all*.

I don't know what I'm expecting when we get there, but the sprawling buildings we pull up to aren't it. Inside, I'm surprised at the rich, earthy colours as we make our way through the halls.

The intake makes my head spin. They check me for contraband and then give me some T-shirts and sweat-clothes. I also get a hygiene pack with travel-size toiletries. A counsellor goes over a bunch of rules and stuff, but I barely hear her. When she's done she gives me a booklet and tells me it's all in there if I forget anything.

There are six other girls in the unit I'm in and I might as well admit that I'm scared to death when I first meet them. Luckily, we each have our own room, which includes a sink and toilet. Showers are private, too, in separate rooms on the unit.

As relieved as I am by those things, everything feels strange and I can't calm the queasiness in my stomach. I tell myself over and over that I won't be there long, that Karan will have me out by the next day.

It doesn't quite work out that way. I end up being there for over a week. At least it's a relief to discover that the staff are not what I expected. They're firm, but they treat us pretty decent, and I feel safest sticking close to them when I can.

Of the other girls on the unit, three seem okay, but one named Jade acts like she has something to prove. The other two ignore me, which is fine with me. I keep to myself as much as I can and walk through the days like a zombie. At mealtimes I can hardly force myself to eat. The night is the worst. I lay awake for hours feeling more alone than I've ever felt before.

I keep from feeling sorry for myself, or giving in to despair, with thoughts of the little girl and her family. I now know that her name was Suzie Quian. It's all over the news, but I can't stand to watch it. I don't want to see her picture — probably a school photo, smiling out at me from a TV screen, and I sure don't want to see her family or the grief on their faces.

It's strange how guilty I feel. I'm haunted by the thought of that little girl, Suzie, lying cold and still forever. The image of her face at the moment she came into the store is imprinted on my brain. I expect it will always be there.

Much of the time it feels like a bad dream, something I'll wake up from with that huge sense of relief you get when you realize a nightmare isn't real. I keep telling myself over and over that it was Devlin, that I wasn't involved. I need to, with the media reporting that the police are closing in on the shooter and a female accomplice has already been arrested.

It takes less than a day for the girls on the unit to put it together — the timing of the killing and my arrival there at Burnaby. They ask me if I was the one who was with the guy who shot Suzie Quian. I turn away from the question, which is all the answer they need.

They push for a while but when I refuse to talk about it they finally let it drop. Even so, on the fourth day I'm there, Jade tells me that I don't deserve to live.

Chapter Twenty

Nine numbing days pass before I find myself being transported to the courthouse for a bail hearing. My dad is there, along with Andrea, whose phony face is putting on a big show of being supportive. As if. She'd probably like nothing better than to have me out of the way.

"We're here for you, Lexie," she says when they get to speak to me for a few minutes before court. "No matter what you've done, we're still family."

"What do you mean, 'no matter what I've done,'" I say, barely keeping myself under control. She's lucky my hands are cuffed or I might not be able to keep from grabbing her by her scrawny neck.

"Now, Lexie, Andrea didn't mean that the way you're taking it," Dad says, on her side as usual. Why he can never see through that two-faced creature is beyond me.

Now isn't the time to get into it, though. I don't suppose the judge will be impressed if I create a big commotion just outside the courtroom.

I hardly understand anything that's being said when they start talking about me. Karan gives me a quick nod and smile when it's over and, thankfully, I find out I'm allowed to go home until we go to trial.

At the house I go straight to my room. It feels like the best place in the world. Weariness rolls over me like a wave and I sink onto the mushroom-coloured duvet that covers my bed. Pressing my cheek into my pillow is the last thing I remember until Barb comes to get me for dinner.

She looks frightened as she tells me it's time to eat. I wonder what they've told her to make her so nervous.

"Do you know why I was away?" I ask.

Barb looks at the floor.

"Did Dad tell you where I was?" I persist.

"He said you had to go somewhere for a while. That's all."

I study her face for a few seconds. She looks like she might cry.

"Barbie," I say gently, "I think someone else told you something about where I was. If you tell me what you heard, I promise I'll tell you if it's true or not."

Her eyes fill with tears. "The kids at summer group said bad things," she says.

"What kind of bad things?" I try to hide the anger I feel.

"They said you shot a girl with a gun."

"Do *you* think that's true?" I'm wondering, as we talk, why no one in the house noticed that my sister was carrying around this huge burden. It's not like Barb is hard to read — when something troubles her, we all know it.

"I *told* them they were liar, liar, pants on fire, but *they* said that's why you were gone. They said you were in jail for shooting that girl with a gun."

Now she's sobbing and I cross the room and put my arms around her. "It isn't true, Barbie. You were right — you're smarter than them because you knew the truth, no matter what they said."

"You didn't shoot a girl with a gun?"

"No, honey. Of course not. I was there when it happened, but I didn't do it."

"Did you *see* the girl getting shot?" Her eyes widen behind the tears.

"Yes." The image trails through my head in slow motion. The door opening, the young girl — Suzie — coming in, Devlin turning, startled by the sound and movement. I flinch as the sound of the shot blasts through my memory.

"But you didn't do it?"

"I promise you, I didn't."

"Then why did you have to go away?"

"It's hard to explain that part," I say slowly. We've always told Barb that she could tell the police if she ever needed help. I don't want to ruin that by saying the wrong thing.

"Some people made a mistake and thought I was part of it, that I did something wrong too," I continue. Barb is watching me closely. "But later on I'm going to get a chance to tell what really happened."

"Then everyone will know you didn't do it?"

"Yes, then they'll know," I say. I give her another hug and meet her smile with one of my own. Sometimes I envy how simple things are for her.

Everyone else is at the table when we get there and I slide into place next to Lynne. She doesn't look at me.

"Hey, Lynne," I say. I try to make my voice cheerful even though I'm hurt that she seems to be ignoring me.

"Hi." Her answer is flat and cold.

"Who made dinner?" I ask, knowing it was Lynne. It's a chicken-vegetable stir fry and basmati rice, Dad's favourite. She makes it a lot.

"Lynne," Barb says. "I helped! I rinsed the snow peas and bean sprouts for her, right Lynne?"

"You sure did," Lynne says with a smile for Barb.

"It looks great," I say. Lynne doesn't answer. I give up and eat in silence while Dad starts talking about a bunch of everyday things, as if this is just a normal day. He doesn't seem to realize that his voice is too loud and cheerful to be convincing. I don't care. It's better than silence, which is apparently what I'm going to get from Lynne.

I try to talk to her after dinner is over and the chores are done, but she cuts me off, goes to her room, and closes the door.

There's nothing I can do but wait until she's ready to tell me what's bothering her.

Chapter Twenty-One

This might sound strange, but there's one thing I'm dreading even *more* than the trial and that's school. No matter how often I try to tell myself that it will be okay, my stomach hurts at the thought of having to go there and face everyone I know.

How many of them will believe I'm guilty? I hope my friends will stand behind me, but what about the hundreds of kids I know from being in classes together over the years?

There's almost no time to prepare myself, either. The September semester starts just four days after I get home from Burnaby. I spend a lot of that time sleeping and avoiding talking to anyone who calls. Except for a few conversations with Dori, I've spoken to no one outside the house.

I tell Dad I don't think I can do it. He listens, but later he and Andrea sit me down and give me a very unhelpful speech about facing your problems. It's clear they're not going to budge on the subject.

I'm still getting the silent treatment from Lynne most of the time. That hasn't changed when I sit down at the breakfast table that Tuesday morning. After giving me an icy glance, she pretends to be super-interested in her breakfast.

There are grapefruit halves and cinnamon toast piled on plates, but the thought of eating makes me nauseous. I make a cup of tea and sip it while Barb, hyped up for the first day of school, chatters about her new outfit.

"My friend Polly said I better not wear the same thing as her," she giggles at one point. "Polly likes Duane, you know. He has freckles. Last year she tried to kiss him!"

This goes on until I can't take it any longer. I tell Barb, "Will you *please* stop talking for a minute! You're making my head hurt."

The silence is instant. So is my remorse. "I'm sorry," I say quickly, "I'm just nervous about school today."

Barb takes her plate and moves around the table to sit beside Lynne. She seats herself sideways on the chair so she's turned away from me.

"Very nice," says Lynne, like she's never been impatient with Barb in her whole life.

I feel as though I can't quite breathe. Maybe some fresh air will help. I pick up my cup and go down the hallway toward the front door. Except, voices in the living room stop me. Dad and Andrea, speaking quietly, are talking about me.

"I don't know why you always insist on taking her side," Andrea is saying.

"Be reasonable," my Dad tells her. "This is really hard for Lexie. I just think we could cut her some slack if she wants to wait a week or so."

"If she *wants* to wait," Andrea says with a sharp laugh. "I'm surprised she hasn't manufactured some phony illness to get out of it. You can be sure that if you give her the choice, she'll jump on it. But, you're just giving in to her. As usual."

As usual? I can't believe my ears!

"I'm sick of arguing with you about the girls," Andrea goes on. "It's no wonder they have no respect for me — you never back me up."

"I back you up all the time," Dad says. His voice is very calm and quiet, the way it gets when he's really angry.

"In front of them, maybe," she says. "What good is that when we argue about them the rest of the time?"

I'm stunned. From the day my father married her, I've always thought he agreed with Andrea on, well, just about everything. Now I find out that he actually sticks up for us — a lot by the sound of it.

"Don't worry, Andrea, I'm not *going* to fight about this," Dad says. "Lexie has been through a lot lately. If she doesn't feel she can face school right now, I'm not forcing her to go."

"Then you might as well just tell her to stay home," Andrea snaps. "There's no way she'll go if she doesn't have to and you know it. I'm telling you, you're giving her the wrong message."

I back up slowly, and then hurry to my room. Sitting on the edge of my bed I try to calm the feelings jumping around in me. I'm happy — *so* happy, that my dad defended me. And I'm almost weak with relief to know that he's not going to make me go to school after all.

Of course, I have to look surprised when he tells me — so I take some deep breaths, finish my tea, and then go back to the kitchen and nibble on a piece of toast while I wait for him to tell me the good news.

It's only a few moments before he and Andrea come into the room. They sit together across the table and then out it comes.

"Andrea and I have decided that we may have been a little harsh when you asked about missing some school," Dad says. Andrea forces a thin-lipped smile, as if she agrees. "So, we're going to leave it up to you — for now, anyway. If you really don't think you can deal with school right now, then we won't force you to go."

I'm about to tell him "thanks" when the expression on Andrea's face stops me. She looks like a cat, about to pounce, and I know she can hardly wait to get my dad alone so she can point out that she was right. In a flash, I decide that's not going to happen.

"Thanks, Dad," I say, "but I think I can handle it. And anyway, I might as well get it over with now. It's not going to be easier later on."

Dad and Andrea look just about as surprised as I feel. But that's not all. Dad starts swelling with pride. I mean it — his chest is literally expanding and there's a goofy smile on his face.

Even Andrea is shocked into niceness. "Well, my goodness!" she says. "That's very responsible of you, Lexie."

"Thanks," I say, wondering how much I'm going to regret this later.

"If you'd rather avoid the bus — at least in the mornings," Andrea continues, "I can drop you off."

"Uh, I'll see how it goes," I say. "Thanks for the offer, though."

And the truth is, the bus ride is okay. No one seems to be paying much attention to me. Maybe this won't be so bad after all.

Chapter Twenty-Two

I should have known better.

It starts almost as soon as I get to school. At first it's whispers. Faces close together, hands over mouths, curious eyes turned toward me. Conversations that trail off as I get near and then buzz back to life as I pass by.

I act like I don't notice. I hold my head up and push through the wave of stares and words. I tell myself they'll lose interest soon enough. After all, there are new classes to find, friends to reconnect with — all the busy, first-day-of-school things to distract them.

But it doesn't happen that way. The whispers grow louder. By noon there are comments that can only be deliberate, and meant for me to hear.

Jumbles of words and phrases come to me, sent by angry, judging mouths. The word "murderer" makes its way through more than once. I want to run through the halls and out the door. I would have, too, if it wasn't for Dori.

"I wonder how dumb these morons will feel when the truth comes out," she says loudly, more than once. Her eyes flash and her face is defiant, challenging anyone who has the nerve to come and say something directly. No one does. Even so, it's gotten to me.

"I don't think I can do this," I tell her.

"You have to. If you go home and hide, it will look bad — like you're guilty and can't face anyone. You've *got* to tough it out, Lex."

I know she's right. Oddly, I find myself thinking about some of the things they used to say in meetings at New Valley.

This is where I am today, I tell myself, *It takes time to get better*. I'm not sure why, but repeating those lines to myself seems to help a little.

Somehow, I get through the day. And I keep telling myself that it will get easier, but Wednesday is worse. There is growing aggression in the looks and comments that come my way. I can't even describe what it's like to have that much anger and hatred directed at you for something you know you didn't do.

My stomach rebels at the thought of dinner that night and I'm barely able to force down a few tiny bites. Lynne shocks me when she says she'll do my chores if I want to lie down.

I'm in my bedroom when she appears in the doorway.

"I'm sorry," she says without looking at me, "for the way I've been acting."

"It's okay," I say, "but why have you been so angry with me? You don't think I had anything to do with —"

"No. Of course not." She pauses, then comes in and sits on the edge of the bed. "It's just that a lot of kids are giving me a hard time about it. And I don't know why you had to go back out with Devlin in the first place."

"I thought he was getting better," I say. It sounds weak and lame and I feel foolish even saying it.

"Well, he wasn't. And our whole family is paying for it."

"I'm sorry, Lynne. I really am."

Then, before we can talk about it any more, Dad comes to the doorway. "Your lawyer just called, Lexie. They've arrested Devlin."

"Yes!" Lynne yells. She gives me a hug.

I smile at her, but it's hard to feel elated. It's not like a happy ending by any means.

I plead a headache, and, once alone, lie down with the light out and blind drawn. Devlin, arrested, locked up. I don't suppose he'll find the whole withdrawal scene quite the same in jail as he did at New Valley. There will be no support staff, no comfy bed or soft pillow, no meds to help him through it, no consideration for his misery. Not that I have much sympathy for whatever he might suffer.

I wonder when, and under what circumstances, I'll see him again. Will it be when we get to court? But maybe I won't have to go now. Karan told me that once they get Devlin and hear what he has to say, they could drop the charges against me. Apparently, that will depend on what other evidence they have.

I'm not one bit worried about that. Since the whole case against me is a misunderstanding, I can't imagine they'll push it once he tells them the truth.

So, I should be relieved, but all I feel is empty and tired. I want this to be over with. I want my life back.

I want Suzie Quian to have *her* life back.

Chapter Twenty-Three

"Devlin has given the police a statement," Karan tells me. "Unfortunately, it implicates you in the crime."

It's the next afternoon and I'm at Karan's office with Dad. He's asked us to come in to discuss things, but this isn't at all what I was expecting to hear.

"Implicates me?" I echo. "You mean he said I was involved? On purpose?"

Karan flips through some papers on his desk. "According to Devlin, the robbery was actually your idea. And he says it was your suggestion that he use you as a pretend hostage."

"Well, that's ridiculous," Dad says, which is a good thing, because I can't seem to make my mouth work. "Surely they don't believe him."

"They want two convictions," Karan tells us. "And they figure his testimony will help them get that."

"But why?" I cry, finally finding my voice. "Why would he *say* those things?"

Karan shrugged. "For a plea bargain — reduced charge. And don't forget that Devlin is a junkie. They could have gotten him to co-operate for a few candy bars."

"But he's lying!"

"The point is, Lexie, we have to deal with what's in front of us. And it doesn't look good."

"Because a *drug addict* gave a statement?" Dad asks. His voice is deep and angry.

"I'm afraid there's more than that," Karan says. "For one thing, the clerk in the store basically says the same thing — that you and Devlin were clearly in cahoots."

I think back to that horrible day. "I know the woman who was working there got that idea," I say. "He cut me when he was pressing the knife against my throat. So, of course I told him to be careful. What would you do if someone had a knife to your throat?"

Karan listens without reacting to what I'm saying. I wonder if he even believes that I'm innocent.

"Witnesses at your job, including a co-worker named Paula, all say that you walked out on your shift at work and joined him just before the robbery. But the most damaging thing is the videotape."

"The videotape?" I say.

"The store has a surveillance camera. There's a videotape of you and Devlin entering the store together."

"Have you seen it?" Dad asks. He doesn't look at me.

"I have a copy right here," Karan says. He lifts a remote and points it at the wall. Panels open revealing a big-screen TV. Another click and images begin to play.

They're a little blurry, but the two people coming through the doorway are definitely Devlin and me. My heart sinks as I realize how bad it looks — the two of us talking to each other. Anyone could easily think we're discussing what we're about to do.

"I was trying to talk him out of it," I say weakly.

And then I watch in horror as Devlin leans down and kisses my cheek.

Karan lets it play another few minutes, while Devlin and I continue to talk and then move toward the front of the store.

"What about the part of the actual robbery?" Dad asks.

"That camera wasn't working," Karan says. He doesn't sound like he thinks that was a bad thing.

"So, this is what we're dealing with here," Karan goes on. "The police have statements from Devlin, the store clerk, Lexie's co-workers, and a couple of customers, and they have the videotape."

"What do we have?" Dad asks.

"We've got Lexie's word. Of course we'll maintain that Devlin and Lexie are arguing on the videotape, but the kiss doesn't help."

I can hear it in his voice. We have virtually no defence. All of the evidence is against me, and the one person besides me who really knows the truth has sold me out for a lighter sentence.

"The problem is," Karan continues, "a little girl died. Any jury in the country is going to want to see someone pay for that. But we can avoid that if we don't go to trial, which is my recommendation."

"What do you mean?" I ask.

"I mean, we offer them a guilty plea in exchange for a reduced charge. You weren't the shooter, so I think I can get them to go for —"

"Hold it right there!" my father says. His face is flushed. "Is this what we're paying you for? I thought you were going to *defend* Lexie — if that's not the case, tell me right now and we'll get someone else."

Karan holds up a hand and says, "It's my job to tell you what your options are. If you want to go to court, that's fine, but we're dealing with a homicide here, and you need to know what the risks are if we go to trial and lose. I'll give Lexie the best defence possible, but there's a lot of circumstantial evidence against her. And you can never predict what a jury will do. "

I sit silently while he and my dad discuss it. It's like I'm not even there but that doesn't matter — I can't get anything clear in my head, anyway.

I feel strangely and utterly alone.

When the decision is made to go ahead, to go to trial and face a jury, it barely registers.

Chapter Twenty-Four

One thing about reaching a really low place in life is you start to think about things in a new way.

I think about freedom these days. Never gave it a thought before, what it means to be free. The short time I spent inside the youth centre in Burnaby really made me aware of how much you lose when you lose your freedom.

Of course, you can't come and go the way you normally would. Want to enjoy the sunshine, take a little walk? Go shopping, meet up with friends? Forget it.

But, the big part of it isn't about what you can't do, or where you can't go. A lot of it is what you have to do. Someone else is making all your decisions. When and what you eat. What you watch on TV, how loud it is, when it's turned off. What you wear. What time you go to bed, and what time you get up. When you shower.

All of your choices are taken away.

Thinking about having to live that way for who-knows-how-long if I get sent away is something I just can't deal with right now. I try not to let it creep into my thoughts, but I can't always help it.

I don't know how I'd be able to stand it if I couldn't see my sisters and my dad all the time. Even Andrea doesn't seem so bad lately. Not that this has made us particularly close, but there are some small changes.

Ditto for friends, especially friends like Dori. But there's someone else who proves to be a friend in a pretty surprising way.

It's Karan who lets me know about it, with a phone call one afternoon.

"Had a visit from a friend of yours," he says. "Could be important."

I'm puzzled, and listen in surprise as he explains.

"Oscar Lee stopped by my office a while ago. Wanted to know if he could help."

"Oscar? What could he do?"

"Testify, actually. You used to date Oscar, is that right?"

"Yes."

"Well, he told me about an evening when he was at your place, and Devlin came over. Do you remember that happening?"

"I remember."

"Devlin asked you for something?"

"A ring. He'd given it to me for my birthday when we were still dating. He asked for it back and I gave it to him. I knew he wanted it for drug money so there was no point arguing."

"Exactly what Oscar said."

"But how does that help? I mean, what good will it do in court?"

"It helps establish a bit of a pattern — how Devlin controlled you, and how he used you to get money for heroin. We needed this — really needed it, and this guy came through for you."

It's a ray of hope. I cling to it, knowing how weak our defence is. I take a few days to gather up enough courage, and then I call Oscar.

"Lexie?" he sounds surprised to hear my voice.

"I just wanted to thank you, for going to my lawyer that way."

"It just seemed like the right thing to do," he says. "Besides, I know you didn't do what you're accused of. It must be pretty awful, going through this."

"It's horrible," I agree, "but this really helps."

"Good then," he says. "Well, I have to go. I have, uh, a friend coming over soon and I need to get my algebra done first."

It doesn't take much brain power to figure out that the "friend" is his new girlfriend. I wish I could tell Oscar that I know I made a terrible mistake, but it would be awkward, and he might take it the wrong way. So I just tell him thanks again and goodbye.

Over the next few weeks, Karan goes over and over my testimony with me. He asks me tough, mean questions to prepare me for what the Crown prosecutor will likely ask. We haven't actually decided if I should take the stand, but with so little in my favour my father thinks I should. Dad believes that if the jury hears my side of the story, they'll know I'm innocent. I'd like to think he's right, but things haven't exactly gone my way lately.

My schoolwork suffers as the date draws closer, but at least I'm sticking it out. My decision to keep going has more to do with needing to be busy than anything else, and I'm glad I haven't given up. Something has shifted at school. The nasty looks and hurtful comments come less often all the time. I can't help but wonder if Oscar has been defending me there, too. I suspect he has, but I can't bring myself to ask him. All I know for sure is that the talk died down after a while, and more and more kids have stepped up to let me know they believe in me. It all helps.

As the trial draws closer, I have trouble sleeping. By the time the date arrives I wonder if my thin, pale appearance will make me look guilty to a jury.

Chapter Twenty-Five

We lose the most important battle before the trial even starts. The court has decided that, because the crime is so serious, I will be tried as an adult. When Karan explains that I could get as much as twenty-five years in prison I wonder if we should have made a deal.

The prosecutor speaks first. She describes the crime — a robbery and homicide. Then she tells the jury that the evidence will prove my guilt beyond a reasonable doubt. She talks about what the evidence will be. And, she wraps up her opening remarks by saying that the defence will try to confuse them but that she is counting on them to see through that and find the truth.

All through the first day I sit numbly while witness after witness takes the stand. Evidence is presented from the emergency workers. The police who were first on the scene describe what they saw. There is medical testimony about the victim — where the bullet went in and how she died. Some members of Suzie Quian's family are there and I hear them sobbing quietly. It is so horrible.

Someone takes the stand to talk about the bullet and the gun. I can't understand why this has to be discussed. It seems as though some of the jury members are bored by the end of that testimony. Everyone is glad when the judge calls it a day.

My father wants to know why Karan hasn't asked many questions of the witnesses that day. Karan explains that we are not challenging that a crime was committed, so we don't need to prove any of that evidence was wrong. We just need to prove that I was not involved in the crime.

I sleep very little that night.

On the second day, two of my co-workers from Subway tell the court that I looked perfectly normal when I left work to join Devlin that day. Not upset, not pressured, just normal. Karan does his best with them. He gets them both to admit that they really don't know anything about my personal life, which makes it unlikely that I would confide in them about the problem I was dealing with. He also tries to plant the idea that someone who is about to commit a crime probably *would* look a bit distressed, not calm, as they've described me.

Officer Neally is next. Her testimony makes it sound like I kept changing my story, so I come across as a big liar. Karan does his best to swing things around with her, but he makes very little headway.

The most damaging testimony comes from the store clerk. She glares at me the whole time she's on the stand. Worse than that, some of the things she says are complete lies. I don't know if she invented them on purpose, or if she's confused, or if someone put ideas in her head, but it's bad. She claims that I was smirking when Devlin had the knife to my throat. Even worse, she says that I told Devlin to "stick her" just before he sent the knife flying into her shoulder.

Karan spends a lot of time cross-examining her. He tries every way he can to get her to say it's possible that I was being forced to be there, but she doesn't budge an inch.

I'm wondering how much worse it can get when the prosecutor wheels in a television to show the jury the store's surveillance tape. I watch helplessly as we enter the store. The images aren't sharp enough to show much expression, but it's clearly me and Devlin. I see him lean forward as we speak to each other. When he bends his head and kisses me on the cheek I see two of the jury members shake their heads a little.

I have to admit that if I were on the jury, I would vote for a guilty verdict. I wonder if it's too late to change my plea and take a deal. Karan told me I could probably get off with eight years. It sounded like forever when he said it, but it's looking pretty good compared to twenty-five.

I'm trying to sort out what to do when Devlin is called to the stand. He strides forward looking determined and almost happy. I guess he feels good about what he's about to do, which is to make himself look as innocent as he can while he throws me under the bus. I can't even stand to look at him when he puts his hand on the Bible and swears to tell the truth. Except that, to my utter astonishment, that's exactly what he does.

It takes a moment or two before it really registers. He's admitting to everything. He describes how he held my arm behind my back, and how it was his idea and that I had nothing to do with it. He describes our conversation before he kissed my cheek, explaining what was really happening on the videotape. When he gets to the part about the shooting, tears run down his face. He sobs as he tells Suzie Quian's family how sorry he is for the terrible pain he caused them. And he admits that the statement he gave to the police was all a lie, that he made it up because he was in withdrawal and desperate.

I'm not the only one who's surprised by Devlin's testimony. The prosecutor is clearly shocked, although she can't stop him. Then the judge asks Devlin why he didn't change his story before now.

"Because," he says, "I knew this was the only way I could see Lexie, and try to tell her, face-to-face, how truly sorry I am. And to ask her to forgive me. She's innocent and she shouldn't even be sitting here today. I'm the one who did it — the only one."

His face is white and full of sorrow as he looks across the courtroom to where I'm seated. His eyes plead for forgiveness.

I nod, ever so slightly. He has enough of a burden to carry. And now, whatever deal he made is off the table. He will be facing the maximum sentence for his crime.

On the other hand, the charges against me are dropped. Suddenly, it's over and I am free to go.

I am grateful. But I've learned something about freedom that goes beyond the matter of where you go and what you eat and wear and so on.

I've learned that the biggest part of freedom comes from inside you. From a clean conscience and an honest heart.

And I know that while I may not have planned a robbery or pulled a trigger, I'm not wholly innocent.

I can never forget the months I spent enabling Devlin, or the fact that the words that first put him on this path, came from my mouth.

"It's nice. Come on, try it."

Acknowledgements

Hearing from readers is one of my favourite things about being a writer! In recent months, the following young people have taken the time to get in touch: Khalil Barakzai, Ryan Carroll, Erica Chen, Stephanie Cook, Katie Cripps, Kylie Cousins, Tia Dayman, Alexi Despres, Connor Doiron, Maddy Doiron, Kelsey Firkola, Lexie Firkola, Kelsey Goudy, Hayley Greening, Stephanie Hauser, Asa Hickey-Ross, Allison Paige Higgins, Emma Hudson, Chelsea Kenny, Daitan King, Abbie Kingston, Chelsea Lavigne, Colin MacDonald, Chandler McIntyre, Chad Nash, Brayden Pachal, Alyssa Pineau, Sidney Potts, Sephora Reid, Aziz Shafqat, and Hasan Shafqat. Thanks to all of you!

Some of the characters who appear in this story were named by or for students. Thanks go out to Nicole Caguiat, Austin Clarke, Ray Li, Oscar Lee, Karan Paralkar, and Dori Wilner for their contributions.

Sixteen-year-old Porter Delaney has his future figured out, but his nice, neat plans are shaken when a man he believes may be his father suddenly appears in his Toronto neighbourhood. Porter knows that he wants nothing to do with the deadbeat dad who abandoned him and his sister twelve years earlier, but curiosity causes him to re-examine the past. Unfortunately, actual memories are scarce and confusing, and much of what he knows is based on things his mother told him. As Porter looks for answers, it begins to seem that all he's ever going to find are more questions.

**Three Million Acres
of Flame**
978-1-550027-273
$12.99

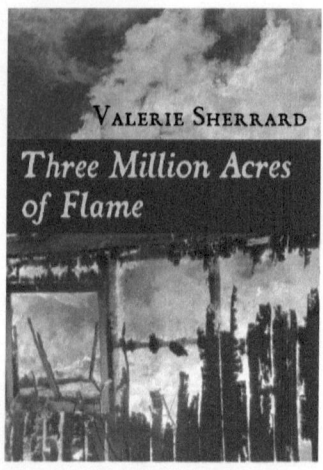

The year 1825 turned
the lives of the Haverill
family upside down.
Following the death of
their mother, Skye and
her brother, Tavish,
have adjusted to living with a single parent. And
when they're asked to make another adjustment
— when their father remarries and his new wife
becomes pregnant — Skye finds that some changes are too much to handle. But family struggles
quickly become irrelevant when the Haverills and
their community are caught up in the Miramichi
Fire, the largest land fire in North American history.

Speechless
978-1-550027-013
$12.99

When his teacher announces that it's time for the yearly class speeches, Griffin Maxwell starts to sweat. His past experience with the dreaded speech was humiliating, to say the least, and he just knows there's no way he can go through that again. So Griffin's best friend, Bryan, comes up with a solution — one that's so simple it just has to work. But neither boy can begin to predict the bizarre chain of events that will be set in place when Griffin goes along with the idea.

From squaring off with the school bully to reading a teacher's private letters, Griffin Maxwell will have to face things he never imagined, and all without saying a word!

Available at your favourite bookseller.

 **DUNDURN PRESS**
w w w . d u n d u r n . c o m

What did you think of this book?
Visit **www.dundurn.com** for reviews, videos, updates, and more!

www.ingramcontent.com/pod-product-compliance
Lightning Source LLC
Chambersburg PA
CBHW022020170626
46808CB00003B/1002